The Secret Vampire

Sarah Emambocus

Published by Sarah Emambocus, 2022.

THE SECRET VAMPIRE

First edition. April 19, 2022.

Copyright © 2022 Sarah Emambocus.

ISBN: 979-8201514211

Written by Sarah Emambocus.

Table of Contents

This book is dedicated to Sarah Shah who has always inspired and encouraged me to fly towards my dreams and believing in me.

Chapter 1

All town have a secret, all town have a past. Who knew the past would one day repeat itself? 10 years ago, in Cape town. Vampires' population was high. No humans were safe. Human and Vampires were enemies in the town as the Vampires were ruled by the vampire king and queen over the town. The humans were getting tired of not being able to leave their homes at night; too scared to do anything because of the Vampires everywhere anytime ready to kill or feed on them.

The Mayor of Cape Town who was human chose to declare war against the vampire. The Vampire King was not happy with that.

The day the human attacked the Vampires were ready, and the fighting started. Every attack the humans made the Vampire took them out. The town was a bloodbath. As the weeks went on more humans died; Vampires were too powerful. Humans were plotting a secret weapon. The Human used garlic bombs and holy water however Vampires were quick and stealthy in making sure they avoided the weapons.

The flight was getting bloody and filled with bloodshed everywhere. The humans had the secret weapon as they used a giant garlic bomb aiming for the sky and holy water to the Vampires. It seemed like the humans were winning the war as many of the Vampires either died or retreated. The weather had changed over Cape Town from a stormy rain to sunshine; the humans could feel the victory and that soon the Vampire King would have no choice but to submit to a peace agreement and also managing the remaining Vampires to either live in peace that means 'No hunting and no biting'.

As this was all happening A young man was seen running away from the chaos; however, he was still being chased by a fast unknown spirit just then he slipped and hit his head. He opened his eyes for a moment before blacking out and falling unconscious. Who was he? What was the figure that was chasing him? why was he running?

Chapter 2

As the unknown guy was running away, he slipped and hit his head; he opened his eyes briefly seeing two shadow figures before he closed his eyes. 'I am really dead'. A few moments later he awakes as he looks around the surrounding. It is old style decorations. The guy tries to look at his reflection in the mirror but does not see one. The curtains are drawn as he tries to remember what happened; just then a voice calls him" Come downstairs". The guy is worried and wonders 'where am I? what is this place?'. As he comes downstairs, he sees two people a heavily pregnant woman who is wearing a very long old dress and crown and a guy who looks atleast over 100 years but isn't showing old age. He also wears a crown; the guy says" who are you?". The King replies" I am the Vampire King Vlad, and this is my wife Carmilla". The guy says" ok but why am I here? I was...." Vlad replies; " dead. You are dead. You will be our son, our legacy". The guy was shocked" Who am I?". Carmilla feels pain as Vlad tends to his wife and calls the doctor.

The doctor delivers the baby which is a girl however Carmilla passes away. The unknown guy holds the baby in his hand as she opens her eyes revealing red eyes. Vlad says" my love don't leave me!". Vlad bites Carmilla's neck as Carmilla opens her eyes. The doctor who is human says" you are all Vampires." As she tries to flee frightened; Vlad says" Callum get her". he corners as she pleads however, he bites her heavily draining her. Vlad kisses Carmilla and says" we have our little princess and our prince." Vlad says to the guy; "You will be known as Callum". Callum wipes the blood from his mouth as Vlad says to his servant; "Dispose of the body". Callum eyes changes from blue to red.

Six years pass as back to the present Cape town has changed since many years ago; a new family is due to move in. They are called the Rodriguez family. As the house has already been setup, a young woman is arranging a room as someone comes in and says" Cel come on!" The young woman comes down from the step ladder and says" Ok Bri I am coming". Celeste comes into the kitchen where her dad Elijah says" Celeste sweetie come and eat". Celeste sits down as Brianna eats the pizza. Brianna says" dad wouldn't have started without you." Celeste took a bite as she tried to swallow it, she then looked around the house but didn't find photos of them all together. Elijah says" you two must be excited to start a new school." Brianna was twelve years old and was happy however Celeste was eighteen and not as ecstatic. Elijah noticed Celeste was distracted as he asks" are you ok?". Celeste said" why is mom's not picture up?". Elijah says" Celeste just eats your food". Celeste says" no I want to know!". Elijah screams" GO TO YOUR ROOM!" Brianna gets scared as Celeste grabs her jacket and heads out. As she comes out and walks into town, she doesn't know why but feels something strange. Celeste sees the forest and decides to go however a car comes as she is crossing the road. Celeste freezes as she closes her eyes however just then someone pulls her away.

As Celeste opens her eyes, she sees the unknown guy walking away. A small crowd gathers and helps Celeste as they ask if she is ok. Celeste thinks: 'Who was that?". Back in the castle Callum comes in as Carmilla says" son you have come home." Vlad says" Elise's training is going very well." Callum says" Dad". Vlad says" I have some news to share with you. you will be attending College as a new student in the next few days". Callum says" why do I have to be around the humans?". Carmilla says to Vlad; " he will be taking over soon". Vlad says" we need to still keep up appearances making sure no one suspects us". Callum sighed as he agreed to go. Celeste came home as she thought about the mystery guy.

Chapter 3

A few days go by as Celeste and Callum prepare for their first day of college. The day finally arrived as Celeste was excited as Callum was least thrilled. He didn't want to go however Vlad told him to. Celeste got to the college early as she was elected head of the debate society team. She also managed to obtain a soccer scholarship; About an hour later Callum got to the school as he saw Celeste in the soccer field kicking the ball around. Celeste kicked it hard as it almost hit Callum; Celeste runs over to apologies as she says" I am so sorry um......", Callum looks at Celeste and says" I'm Callum". Celeste extends her hand as Callum walks away as Celeste thinks" what a rude brat!". For some reason Celeste couldn't get Callum out of her thoughts.

After a long day of school Celeste came home as she was still thinking about Callum as she comes to the kitchen as she sees someone there. She knew who it was as she said" Susie". Susie turns around as she has brown eyes, long blond hair, and a cute smile. Susie happily runs to her sister and hugs her as she says" it's good to see you Cel," Celeste and Susie catch up as the nightfall as Susie decides to go for her run. She always enjoyed late night runs. As she runs from the forest pass suddenly someone comes behind her. she stopped as she turned around; the unknown person says "It's dangerous to run here at night". He then disappears into air as Susie is left thinking 'What just happened?'

A few weeks pass by as Susie remembers the incident meanwhile at college both Celeste and Callum become friends. Both Celeste and Callum had deep secrets but didn't share it with each other. One night Brianna was out at her friend's place when she realized it was getting late. Brianna says to her friend Tanya "I have to get going home". Tanya says" I will drop you home." Brianna says" I will be fine." Meanwhile Vlad was out looking for a human to feast on.

Chapter 4

Vlad was looking around for a human to feast on however it was all quiet. Suddenly he saw Brianna coming from a house as he began to follow her. " Who's there?" Brianna asked frightened as there was no response. Vlad jumped down from a tree as a scared Brianna saw him with fangs as she tried to run. Brianna ran into the forest as Vlad who was quicker grabbed her from behind; Vlad bites her neck as Brianna struggled before her body was cold and numb. Vlad bite Brianna draining her of her life before leaving her for dead.

The next day there was no sign of Brianna. She never came home as Celeste decided to call the cops who came over and questioned the whole family. A few days go by, the police find Brianna's body in the woods as Celeste and Susie mourned and cry for their sister. Susie was vengeful and had a deep desire to avenge Brianna's death and says, ' I will find out who killed our baby sister, and they will pay'. Celeste came back to school as she was still grieving but Callum was there supporting her. A few weeks passed by as soon it was Celeste's birthday. She didn't feel like celebrating having lost her sister a few weeks back. Callum went to the Jewelers as he wanted to get a special necklace. The Jeweler says shows a silver chain with a ruby stone. Callum asks" Can you put the necklace on the small cloth?". The jeweler does this as Callum thinks" this is beautiful and would be nice on Celeste's neck." He pays for the necklace and leaves.

The next day is Celeste's birthday as she comes to school as she is by her locker Callum comes behind her as Celeste says" Callum you scared me". Callum apologies as he hands a wrapped box to Celeste wishing her 'Happy birthday'. Celeste takes the box and puts it in her bag as she says" Callum I don't feel like celebrating my birthday'. The bell rings for class as Celeste heads to class. Callum doesn't know why but seeing Celeste sad makes him feel sad. Later that evening after school Celeste comes to the graveyard and places flowers on her sister's grave. Callum watches her from a distance as Celeste cries. She soon comes home as Susie has prepared a delicious meal however Celeste doesn't feel hungry and goes to her room. She empties her bag as the box present falls to the ground. Celeste opens and finds a message ' to the most beautiful girl in the world. Happy birthday Celeste.' She sees a silver necklace with a ruby stone as Celeste thinks ' this is so beautiful'.

Chapter 5

The next day at college, Celeste comes with the boxed gift in a bag as Callum sees her and says, *"hey Celeste you, ok?"*. Celeste says, *"here's your gift back."* Callum takes it as he asks, *" did you not like it?"*. Celeste replies, *"you forgot to put the gift on me."* She takes it out of the box as she gives it to Callum however as Callum's hand touched the silver he screams in pain as there is a cut on his hand. Celeste panics, *"oh no Callum".* Celeste runs to get help as Callum leaves from there; He comes under the bleachers as his scar heals and his red eye softens back to his normal eye color. Celeste comes back with the nurse as she sees Callum has gone.

Callum comes back inside wearing gloves as Celeste sees him and comes to him. Celeste asks, *"where did you disappear to?"*. Callum answers,*" I wasn't feeling well."* Celeste sees Callum in gloves as she says, *"your cut will get an infection".* Callum pins her against the locker as Celeste is scared as he says, *"just leave me alone."* A few days passed by as Callum feels guilty and remorseful of what he did to Celeste. Celeste is playing sports as Callum comes to the stand as he sees her; Celeste sees Callum as she continues to play however one of the girls kicks the ball as it is about to hit Celeste however Callum comes there and pulls Celeste away. Everyone thinks *'how did he get here so fast?'*. Celeste pushes Callum away angrily and says, *"what the hell? first you told me to leave you alone and now you are here."* Celeste storms off angrily as Callum tries to go after her.

Later that evening at the castle Vlad is training with his daughter as Carmilla comes and says, *"where's Callum?"*. Callum comes to his room as Carmilla comes in and says, *"son what is wrong?"*. Callum says, *"I don't want to talk about it mom."* Carmilla says, *"son you haven't fed in a while. Come with me."* she brings Callum to the cellar as he sees someone familiar. Callum recognizes the girl who was about to hurt Celeste. Carmilla says, *"you will feed on her son".* As she was under hypnotism Callum angrily bit into her neck as she screamed before falling. Carmilla says, *"you were only supposed to feed on her not kill her."* Callum with blood over his mouth says, *"she deserved to die."* As he left Carmilla was worried for her son and decided to call the witch.

Chapter 6

L ater that night the witch arrives as Carmilla greets her; Carmilla brings the witch to Callum's room as Callum sees his mom and the unknown person. Callum asks, *"who is this mom?"*. Just as Carmilla is about to reply the witch says, *"I'm Samara and I'm here to help you."* Callum looks at his mom and then says, *"really mom? I don't need a witch or whatever she is."* Callum then went out of the room as Samara and Carmilla talked. Carmilla said, *" I apologies to you on my son's behalf"*. Samara smiles and gives Carmilla a small vial with purple liquid as she says, *"this will help your son be calm and control his vampire powers."* Carmilla thanks Samara as she goes however as Samara leaves, she has an evil smile on her face. At dinner that night Carmilla adds the potion to Callum's drink ; as he drinks it unaware of what is inside, he says *"this taste different and a little funny."* Carmilla says, *"son I am sure it is nothing; we all are drinking the same."* Callum stayed in that evening and did not hunt.

The next day at college, Callum saw Celeste as he came over to her and said, *"hey Celeste"*, she replies, *"hey to you too."* They hug as Callum smells her hair and thinks, *'she smells like lavenders'.* The bell rang as they both talked and went to class; during lunch break Celeste eat inside the canteen as Callum ate with her. *"so, tell me about your family."* Callum's word caught up to his throat as he could not tell her his family were vampires. Callum said, *"my parents have a family business."* Celeste says, *"wow that is amazing, my family is nothing special."* Callum could sense a small sadness in Celeste's face however he did not want to bother her. After school Callum was happy, he felt like jumping and also starting to feel more in control. As he came home, he was happy and relaxed as Carmilla noticed it and smiled. She was so glad Samara had helped Callum and could not wait to see her tomorrow.

The next day Carmilla made her way to the witch's hut. Samara was in a middle of something as she checked and saw Carmilla as she said, *"come in."*, she opened the door and walks in as Samara closes a room. Samara says, *"Queen Carmilla you shouldn't have taken the trouble to come all the way."* Carmilla bows and thanks her for the potion as Samara smiled and replied, *"you're welcome."* As Carmilla left Samara's hut, her face had an evil smirk on her face as she thought *'it's only a matter of time.'* Meanwhile back at Celeste's place Susie was making dinner as their father came home from a long shift. Celeste laid the table as they sat down. Susie said, *"dad I will be leaving soon."* As he looked at her and asked, *"sweetie this is your home."* Susie said, *"this place reminds me of Brianna; her soulless face. I can't..".* Susie gets up and leaves as Celeste looks at her dad who says, *"eat your dinner."*

Chapter 7

The next few days passed by as Susie still thought of Brianna. Celeste asks, *"sis why don't we do something tonight?"*. As Celeste did some research, she found out there was a club across the forest as she said, *"maybe we should head there."* Susie nodded as Celeste and Susie dressed up, they headed into the forest. Callum was with his dad doing training as Vlad said, *"son I think it's time to catch a new meal."* Celeste and Susie got to the club as everyone was dancing and getting drunk; Susie ordered some shots as Celeste got them a table. As Celeste waited for Susie a guy approached her as Celeste noticed he was heavily drunk as he grabbed Celeste's wrist as he tried to pull her however someone came and pushed him to the corner as Celeste got up and saw it was Callum.

Callum said, *"when a girl says no you don't force them asshole!"*. Callum got a glass bottle and smashed it on his head as Celeste looked at him shocked. Susie came back as Celeste was about to leave as Callum held her against the wall as they stared into each other's eye. Celeste asked, *"Callum what did you do?"*. Callum's eye changed color as he held her waist as Celeste was about to scream but Callum said, *"forget what you saw., forget what I did."* Celeste felt strange however she then pushed Callum and slapped him. Callum looked shocked as Celeste said, *"stay away from me!"*. Susie got on the dance floor as Callum came as Susie noticed him and said, *"hey sexyman wanna dance?"*. Callum danced with Susie as Susie grinds on him; Callum then leaves her and heads out. Meanwhile, someone watches Susie as they come over to her however Susie grabs her bag and leaves.

Celeste walks through the forest as Vladimir watches her and thinks *'looks what a delicious human'* . Before he can do anything, Vladimir is pushed against the tree and sees Callum as he says, *"dad you won't feed on her."* Vladimir looked stunned and shocked and said, *"you don't normally protect food."* Callum says, *"she's special and she's mine."*

Vladimir soon flies off as Callum watches Celeste. He makes sure she gets home safe as he thinks *why did the compulsion not work? I need to talk to mom about this.'* The next morning Carmilla is training as Callum says, *"mom I have something to ask."* Carmilla hands him a juice as he drinks it and Callum said, " *I wanted to ask about Vampire mates and compulsion."*

Chapter 8

Carmilla is a little confused as she looks at herdaughter Elise who is training asking, *"honey can you give me and yourbrother a few minutes?".* Elise nods as she runs to get some blood asCarmilla turns to Callum as he says, *"I am not sure about thisson."* Callum frowns as he says, *"I really need to know aboutthis mom."* Carmilla sighed and says, *"I'll look into thistomorrow."* After dinner, Callum went to his room as he studied beforebed. The next day Carmilla went to see Samara who was relaxing and watching amovie as Carmilla came in Samara says, *"what a pleasant surprise!".*As Samara went to get two teas ready; Carmilla sat down as she asked, *"Callumasked me if people can be compelled?"* Samara was confused replying, *"Vampireshave the ability to compel humans, but I will do some research and get back toyou, it may take a few days."* Carmilla nods as she leaves. Samara doesan evil smile as she heads into her secret room.

At school, Callum was reading a book as Celeste walkedpast him. Callum called out, *"Cel can we talk?".* Celeste replied,*"I don't want to talk to you."* As she headed into class; Callum wondered *'doesCeleste know my truth?'.* Celeste was in deep thought as later on that dayCallum pulled Celeste into an empty classroom as Callum said, *"please Celdon't ignore me."* Celeste had tears in her eyes as she said, *"Ijust miss Brianna so much and I feel you are hiding things from me."*Callum hugs her as Celeste feels his warmth as he assures, he is not keepingsecrets. Celeste says, *"promise me you won't keep things from me."* Callum promises as he thinks *'I am sorryCel I am hiding from you a big secret'.* Celeste notices Callum's eyes aretired as she says, *"you look tired?".* Callum replies, *"yeahI didn't get much sleep last night."* Celeste frowns as she said, *"make sureyou get some sleep we have midterms coming up in a few weeks."* Celeste leaves as Callum checks his phone andthinks *'she's right'.* Afterschool, Callum rushed to his room and began to study; everyday until themidterms he kept himself busy.

14

Samara was doing some research into whatCarmilla had asked. Samara thinks *'I may have the answers to all herquestions, but will she be willing to pay the price for it'.* Samara calledCarmilla as she said *"only part vampires and part witches can't becompelled, is Callum a true vampire or is he only a fleshing?".*

Carmilla replies *"he's my son."* Samara rolls her eyes as Carmilla thinks about the girl who Callum had mentioned. Carmilla said *"I have a feeling that Celeste might be hiding a secret."* Samara said, *"well in order to prove things I will need a DNA sample; a piece of her hair is fine."* The next day Callum was on his way to college as Carmilla asks, *"son why don't you invite your friend over?".* Callum said, *"who?."* Carmilla replied, *"Celeste".* Callum said, *"mom I have exams to be worried. I will invite her one day."* As Callum leaves, Carmilla thinks, *'I have to find a way to get her DNA to the witch to check if the girl is special.'* Susie was with Celeste outside college as Celeste felt nervous for tomorrow as it was the midterm exams. Susie said, *"Celeste you've got this."* As Callum comes, he sees Susie and Celeste as Celeste says *"hey"*. Susie winked at Callum as she says *"hey Sexyman."*

Chapter 9

As Celeste sees Susie playfully winking and smirking at Callum; she asks, "*do you two know each other?*". Callum replies *'no'* whilst Susie replies *'yes.'* Susie tells Celeste how he danced with her at the club a few weeks ago. Celeste was stunned as she saw Callum and said, *" I can't believe you didn't tell me."* Celeste goes inside as Susie said, *"what happened?"*. Callum said *"what the hell Susie? Why did you have to tell her for?"*. As Callum heads inside, Susie rolls her eyes and says, *"so much drama."* She soon leaves as in class Callum sees Celeste as he goes to sit next to her, she puts her bag on the chair. Callum said, "*Cel let me explain."* Celeste turns her head away as Callum goes to the back bench as the teacher comes in and says, *" I hope you are ready for your midterms exams."* Callum could not help but stare at Celeste who worked on her exam. After a few hours, the students had a break as Celeste went outside as Callum approached her however Celeste gave him a look and left. Callum thinks *'Cel why can't you give me a chance to explain?'*. The day went by very quickly as Celeste decided to visit Brianna's grave. As she brought some tulips, she placed them on the graveside and talked to her sister about everything and Callum.

Callum watched from a nearby tree as he heard Celeste's words as he felt a pain in his chest and thought *'Cel is in pain'*. As Celeste left; Callum gave to the grave as he said, "*Brianna, I never knew you. but you were the light in Celeste's life; I promise I will protect her."* As Celeste comes to her room, she ignores Susie. Susie barges into Celeste's room as she said, "*don't you think you are overreacting?"*. Celeste yelled, "*SUSIE GET OUT!"*. as Celeste pushed her sister out and locked the door. Susie said, "*I don't need you!"*. Susie stormed out of the house in anger. As Celeste took out a frame photo of her mom, she had tears in her eyes. Celeste never really told anyone why she was so secretive or wanted people around her to be honest; Celeste said, "*mom I miss you so much."* A few hours later Celeste awoke as she heard screaming downstairs as Celeste came downstairs, she saw her dad in a drunk state as he was shouting loudly. *"what is all the shouting about?"*; as Susie replied, *"dad came in drunk, and he's been acting weirdly."* As Susie attempted to smash the bottle; their dad took out his belt as Susie and Celeste looked on shocked. Celeste told Susie, *"upstairs now!"*. Susie said, *"I'm not leaving you sis."* Susie ran upstairs as Celeste took the beating and soon collapsed on the floor.

Callum who was near Celeste's house heard Celeste's scream as he kicked the door down. He came in to see Celeste was unconscious as he saw the man drunk on the floor. Callum's eyes widen in anger as Susie soon came downstairs as she said, *"Cel wake up!"*. Susie said, *"Callum dad beat her so badly."* Callum said, *"I will take care of Cel."* He lifts her and carries her out as Susie said *"atleast take me with you."* Callum said, *"I want to make sure Celeste is ok."* Callum thought, *'I cannot bring her to the castle or the doctors.'* Callum brought her to the forest not too far from the graveyard as he sat down and placed Celeste's head on his lap and wrapped her with a blanket. He watched the moon as he soon closed his eyes; he was unaware, but Celeste's body glowed with a purple light as Celeste stirred and said *'mama'*. Callum awoke for a brief second as he checked Celeste as he stroked her face and said, *"I'm going to take care of you, and I promise you will never face any danger ever again."* Callum soon closed his eyes and slept.

Chapter 10

The next morning Celeste wakes up on Callum's lap as looks around and says, *"what am I doing here?".* As Callum awakes, he says *"good morning how are you feeling now?".* Celeste gets up as she wraps the blanket around her and says, *"why did you bring me here? was it so you could hurt me?".* Callum gets up as he replies, *"something happened last night, and I brought you here away from the doctors who would have asked lots of questions, and also my family is not used to guests."* Celeste takes a breath as she sighs *" you saved me."* Callum nods as Celeste says, *"thanks but that doesn't mean we are on good terms."* Celeste looks around the woods as she sees the graveyard where her sister is buried. Callum says, *"I know it's hard losing a loved one."* Celeste replies coldly *"how would you know? she was my younger sister and had her whole life ahead of her. but because of a monster he snatched her away."* Celeste runs from there as Callum thinks *'I feel what you are feeling Cel. I made a promise to always keep you safe from danger.'* As Celeste comes home, she sees the place has been tidied up as Susie comes down and hugs Celeste as she asks, *"sis are you ok?".* Celeste sits on the sofa as Susie brings a hot tea. Celeste replies *"I am ok."*

As Celeste spends the day resting and in deep thoughts over what happened. In class the next day Celeste sees Callum talking with two guys as she thought *'Callum is not as bad as he seems.'* As Celeste comes to the canteen, she sees Callum as he says, *"hi are you ok?".* She nods as Callum heads upstairs as Celeste comes after him. Celeste sees a flower and a bench as she sees Callum wearing black sunglasses as if he is tanning. Celeste says,*" cool place you have here."* Callum says *" Cel what are you doing here?".* Celeste replies *" I overreacted a few days ago, I am sure you don't hide secrets."* Callum's eyes changed to red in the glasses as he then changed it back to his brown eyes as Callum replied, *" I will be honest and tell you everything now. Could we be friends again?".* Celeste hands Callum a piece of her sandwich as his hands burn and he throws it before running out. Celeste wonders *'why did Callum's hand burn when he held my sandwich?'*. Callum came to the bathroom as he turns on the water however Callum turns it off and looks at his skin which has fully healed.

Celeste comes looking for Callum as he comes out of the men's toilet. Celeste comes to him and says, "*Callum show me your hand.*" Callum says "*Cel I'm fine.*" As Callum shows his hand to her; Celeste does not find a burn or scar as his hand looks normal. Callum hears the bell ring as he said, *"we better head to class."* As Callum walked down the corridor; Celeste was in thoughts as she wondered *'how did Callum's injury heal quickly?'*. Later that evening Celeste was practicing her sports in the college as Callum was at home. Carmilla said *"son you know Halloween is coming up. your dad and I will be out hunting. I think you should have a party."* Callum did not look too interested as Carmilla thinks *'I need this to be a way so that I can get the DNA from the girl.'* Callum eventually agreed as Vlad came and said, "*Callum we need to talk.*"

Chapter 11

As Callum had a quick chat with Vladimir; he soon cameback as Carmilla said "*so it will be Halloween in two days.*"Carmilla was excited and said, "*I can't wait to meet all yourfriends.*" Meanwhile back at Celeste's home she was still thinkingabout Callum injury as she wondered '*a lot of strange things have beenhappening.*' Her thoughts wereinterrupted by Callum's incoming call. Callum said "*hey Cel how areyou?*". Celeste replies "*I am ok. What's up?*". Callumand Celeste chat until it becomes late. Celeste says, " *I'll see you incollege tomorrow.*" Two dayspass quickly as it is Halloween; Celeste is dressed as a butterfly pumpkinprincess. As Callum says, "*everyone is invited to my place for aHalloween party.*" Everyone cheers as they head to Callum's place whichis the castle high on the hill. Celeste comes with the students inside;Carmilla sees Celeste as she thinks '*this must be the girl*'. BeforeCarmilla could approach her; Vladimir called her; Carmilla says "*whatis it darling?*". Vlad answers "*aren't you ready to hunt? Letthe kids have their party.*" Carmilla snaps at Vlad to head out and shewill join soon. Vlad leaves as Carmilla goes to find Celeste as she thinks '*this is the best opportunity to get herDNA*'.

As Celeste was enjoying the party as Carmilla spotted her as Celeste noticed Carmilla looking at her. Carmilla says "*hi sweetie sorry to bother you I was hoping to meet you.*" Before Celeste can reply the lights go out as Carmilla uses this to take Celeste's hair sample. Soon the lights come on as Carmilla has gone; Celeste gets a drink as she notices a mystery guy watching her. The guy approaches Celeste as she asks, "*hi who are you?*" he smiles at her and replies "*hi I'm Gabriel.*" As they shake hands; Celeste and Gabriel dance as Callum watches from a distance and thought '*why am I getting a bad vibe from him?*'. Later on, Gabriel takes Celeste into an empty room as Celeste looks around and says, "*Gabriel why have you brought me here?*". Gabriel closes the door as he says, "*you know you're the most beautiful girl here.*" As Gabriel comes closer to Celeste to kiss her; Celeste pushes him off however as Celeste is about to leave Gabriel pushes her to the bed "*you're gonna give me what I want or else.*" Celeste was scared as Gabriel pinned her arms and began to kiss her neck however the door opened as Gabriel turned around and saw Callum. Celeste says *"Callum".*

Gabriel says, *"oi mate I'm busy here."* As Celeste had tears in her eyes; Callum eyes widen in anger as he started to beat up Gabriel. Callum grabbed his neck and threw him down the stairs as he said, *" how dare you try to hurt Celeste?".* Celeste got up as she ran into Callum's arms as she began to cry. Gabriel yelled, *"this is not over! You will pay for this."* Celeste held her shoulder as Callum noticed a piece of her dress had been ripped. Callum came downstairs and shouted, *"PARTY'S OVER EVERYONE.!".* Callum comes to his room as he takes a shirt and gives it to Celeste to wear.

Chapter 12

As Callum takes Celeste home; Celeste is still thinking *what could have happened if Callum didn't step in?'.* As he drops her off at her house she says, *"thanks for saving me."* As they hug Callum smells Celeste's hair and thinks *'she smells like strawberry and cherry blossom.'* As he says, *"are you sure you'll be, ok?".* Celeste nods as she kisses Callum on the cheek and heads in. Susie sees Celeste in Callum's shirt as she asks, *" what happened?".* The next few days passed quietly as Celeste invites Callum over to her place one night as her dad was doing a night shift at work. Callum says, *"so what are we watching?".* Celeste prepares the popcorn and chicken bites as she replies, *"nightmare on elm street."* As Callum took one of the chicken bites and dipped it in the sauce; he soon spat it out as he says, *"where's the bathroom?".* As Callum heads upstairs and locks the bathroom he turns on the tap to try and clear the taste from his mouth. Callum then came down and says, *"I have to go."* As Celeste tried to stop Callum and ask questions he left. Callum came to the woods as he saw a guy walking and then fed on him.

The next morning Celeste was filled with questions as she came to the college and saw Callum. Callum says *"Cel I know you probably have a lot of questions regarding last night."* Meanwhile, Carmilla made a trip to see Samara with the DNA sample. As Samara took it, she says *" Carmilla I will need a few days to get this checked."* Carmilla nodded and says, *"you can come to the castle when you have found out the results."* As Carmilla left; Samara called out to her son. As he came in front, and it was none other than Gabriel; Gabriel puffed smoke as Samara says, *" I know you didn't do well at the party in seducing the girl."* Gabriel says, *" don't worry mom I have my revenge plan ready."* Back at the college after lessons had finished; Callum spoke with Celeste. Callum says, *"I have an allergy to garlic."* Celeste found it a little strange however she apologized as Callum says, *" you don't need to be sorry."* As the coach called Celeste for training, she went as Callum decided to watch her from the field. Callum thought,' *I know that feelings are getting deeper between us, but I must protect you.*'

Later that afternoon Gabriel came to Celeste as Celeste was shocked to see him and says, *"Gabriel what are you doing here?"*. Gabriel acted apologetic as he says *" I am sorry for the night when I tried to... I was drunk."* Celeste says, *" you're a liar."* Gabriel attempted to manipulate Celeste's memories however Callum came and pushed Gabriel. Celeste held Callum's arm as Callum says, *" Celeste go from here."* Celeste was about to ask questions as Callum says " Go"; she left as Callum's eyes changed to red and he says *"I'm giving you one warning! Stay away from Celeste or else."* Gabriel smirked and replied, *"or else."* As the weather got stormy; Callum clenches his fist in anger and asks; *"are you prepared to find out how far I am willing to go?"*. Gabriel disappears but not before saying *"this is far from over."*

Chapter 13

As Celeste came home, she was worried about Callum; however, as the doorbell rang; she opened to see Callum and ran into his arms. She hugged him as Callum held her and says, *"Cel I'm ok. Sorry I had to use anger to make you go."* Celeste says, *" it's ok I understand."* Callum says, *"I'd better go."* Celeste nods as she waves bye and closes the door. Meanwhile, Gabriel came home to tell Samara of his plan as Samara was busy. Gabriel says, *" that girl is important to Callum."* Samara says, *"son I don't have time for your little games; I have bigger fish to fry."* Gabriel rolls his eyes and leaves as Samara is working on the DNA. Over the next days, it is quite as Celeste is still checking her surrounding as Callum comes to Celeste and asks, *"are you ok?".* Celeste looks at Callum as Callum senses that she is still afraid; Callum places his hand on Celeste and says, *"Gabriel won't try anything and if he does, he won't make it out of here alive."* Celeste smiles and thinks *' Callum is so sweet and protective.'* After college, Celeste went to eat ice cream with Susie as Callum had a family meeting to attend to.

Susie and Celeste sat in the dessert parlour. Susie says, *"so how's sexy man?".* Celeste gave Susie a cold stare as she says, *" Jeez calm down."* As Celeste says, *"Callum has been nice and protective."* Susie sees in Celeste's eyes as it sparkles and says, *" you like him."* Celeste laughs and says, *"we're just friends."* Meanwhile Callum was stuck in a meeting with his dad Vladimir as he thought of Celeste and smiled. Vladimir says, *" son are you listening?".* Callum nods as later that evening Susie is in the club dancing as Callum comes to enjoy. Celeste finishes a drink as she notices Callum as Celeste says *"Callum... Cal.",* Susie spots Callum as Celeste has had a lot to drink. Callum puts her on a sofa as Susie says, *" my sister is such a lightweight when it comes to drinking."* Susie feels Callum is hiding a secret as she says, *" you'd better not hurt my sister."* Callum was a little confused as he says, *" me and Cel are friends."* Susie laughs and says, *"I can see it in her eyes; she likes you more than a friend."* Susie comes closer and says, *"what's your secret Sexy man?"*.

Callum was stunned as he says, *"Susie are you drunk?"*. Callum lifts Celeste in his arms and says, *" I'll take her home."* as Callum carries Celeste out; Celeste talks in her sleep as she says, *"you smell nice... like pinewoods... Callum."* Callum looks around and heads at superspeed to her home. As he places her on the bed; Callum is about to go as Celeste holds his hand as she opens her eyes and says *" Callum."* Callum turns back as Celeste says, *" stay with me Callum; you make me feel safe."* As Callum kisses Celeste's forehead, she falls back asleep as Callum sleeps by her side. The next morning Celeste awakes and sees Callum sleeping beside her as she smiles, however, kicks Callum off the bed as says, *" Callum what the hell?"*. Callum awakes as he sees Celeste as she says, *" I can't believe you slept here."* As Susie opens the door and comes in, she is stunned by what she sees. Susie says, *"you sly fox!"*. Callum says, *"we didn't have sex."* Callum leaves by the window as Celeste wonders, *'could I have misunderstood him again?'*.

Chapter 14

As Callum returns back to the castle; he changes and gets ready for college; As Celeste takes the rest of the day to recover. The next day Celeste comes to class as a guy walks in as all the girl in the class were saying *'he's hot! Who's the mystery guy?'.* Celeste rolls her eyes as Mr Raymond comes in as he says, *"Ah everyone I see you have met Damien our new student; please make him feel comfortable".* As Celeste notices Damien's blue eyes and blond hair; she thinks ' what's so special about him?'. Damien looks for a seat as he sits beside Celeste. Callum comes there and says, *"oi newbie you're in my seat."* Damien says *"listen a seat is a seat. You don't own it."* As Callum clenched his fist angrily; Celeste says *"enough!".* After class Damien says, " thanks for trying to help me out babes but I don't need it." Celeste says, *"please don't call me babes. my name is Celeste."* As a few girls try to talk to Damien; Damien apologises as he asks, *"can you show me around the college?".* Celeste walks away as Damien thinks *'I will get her to talk me around.'*

After the next few classes Celeste still notices Damien is following her as she soon snaps as she says, *"what do you want jerk?";* Damien gets on his knees and sings *"I'm begging, begging you."* As Celeste sees a small crowd gather around her; she sighs and says, *" fine get up?".* Celeste talks with Damien as Callum comes and says *"Cel are you ok?".* Celeste who was still mad at Callum says, *"don't call me Cel."* Damien was confused about the situation as he asks, *"is this your boyfriend?".* Celeste laughs and says, *" we're just friends."* As Celeste says, *" let's go."* Callum looks sadly as Celeste leaves with Damien as she shows him around the college campus. Damien asks, *"what is wrong with the name Cel?".* Celeste rolls her eyes and says, *" It's a special nickname and I don't allow anyone to just call me it."* Later on, at lunch Callum pulls Celeste into the janitor's closet as she says, *" what the hell?".* Callum says *"Cel please talk to me; we didn't have sex. You were drunk and I stayed by your side."* Callum leaves as Celeste is left in deep thoughts.

Meanwhile back in the Witches' hut, Samara was plotting something big against Carmilla's family. *"They will die slowly; first Carmilla, Vladimir and then Callum; no one will survive."* As Samara laughs evilly; she soon got back to investigating the DNA as Samara thinks *'this is unlike any DNA I have ever seen.'* As Samara still works on it; Gabriel comes in as Samara asks, "*Gabriel shouldn't you be out?".* Gabriel replies, "*mom I am bored."* Samara starts to zap him as Gabriel jumps up and down holding his bum screaming as Samara says, " you just wanted entertainment." Gabriel takes a deep breath as he falls to the floor and sighs however as he touches his butt, but he feels burned. Gabriel says, *"MAMA!"* Samara says, *"don't be a baby."* Samara continues to work on the DNA and her evil plan. Back in the castle, Callum was in his room sketching a picture of Celeste as Carmilla knocked on the door as Callum says " come in." Carmilla came with a juice as she asked, "*how are you son?".* Callum was feeling a little sad thinking of Celeste as he drank the juice and got some rest.

Chapter 15

The next day at school Callum was walking down the corridor as he saw Gabriel. Callum rolls his eyes and starts to walk past however Gabriel trips him; Gabriel laughs and says, " *loser.*" Callum looks around as he got up and his eyes changed to red in anger; he grabbed Gabriel's collar and pushed him into the janitor's closet as he locks the door; Gabriel starts knocking as Callum smirks as he leaves. As Celeste is passing, she hears a knock on the door as she opens it and sees Gabriel who comes out of the dark and says, *"thanks for letting me out."* Celeste says, " *who put you in here?".* Gabriel thinks '*I can't tell I wanted to put Callum in here and the plan got backfired'.* Gabriel takes Callum's name as he leaves. Meanwhile, in the library, Callum is studying as Celeste comes and says, *"Callum why did you put Gabriel in the janitor's closet locked up?".* Callum rolls his eyes and says, *"he deserved it."* Celeste wasn't happy as Callum says, *"why do you care about Gabriel all of a sudden?".* Celeste says, *"I don't but there is such a thing called humanity."*

Callum rolls his eyes as he gets up and leaves; Celeste wonders ' *why is Callum acting so cold?'.* As Callum came to the canteen; he saw Gabriel eating as Callum thought about Celeste's words and approached him. Gabriel says, " *if you are back to finish round two."* Callum apologizes as Gabriel is stunned as Callum says, " *look I don't want trouble."* Gabriel leaves as Callum sits and eats his sandwich as he remembers a memory from the past; when he was younger and was at a sleepover; they bullied and teased him as they pushed him into a cold basement. As Celeste has seen Callum apologizing, she thinks ' *maybe I have misunderstood Callum.'* As she comes over; Callum says " *Cel I..."* Celeste says " *I'm sorry for not understanding the situation... I know you would never take advantage of me."* Damien sees Celeste and Callum close as he sees Gabriel and says " *I know what you did earlier to*

Callum. Let's say that Callum pushing you in the closet was only a small punishment." Gabriel says, *"what are you going to do about it?"*.

Damien pushes Gabriel against the locker as he says, *"don't hurt others especially Callum and Celeste."* Gabriel asks, *"why do you care?"*. Damien says, *"they are both my friends and are important to me."* Celeste comes there as Gabriel leaves as Celeste asks, *"hey Damian how are you liking school so far?"*. Damian says, *"it's cool."* As Callum sees Damien and Celeste talking and laughing, he isn't too happy. Damien notices Callum as he hugs him and says, *"look you don't need to worry about Gabriel."* Callum says, *"I am more than capable of sorting out my own troubles."* Gabriel notices Celeste and thinks *'she seems like a sweet girl who knows maybe I can make her fall for me.'* later that afternoon Callum watched Celeste as she was playing sports as he was glad that things had been sorted out; Damien and Gabriel came as Callum wondered *'I know why Damien is here but why is Gabriel here?'*. Gabriel closes his eyes as he chants a spell with his mind as Celeste is about to trip over as Callum goes over and holds her. Celeste opens her eyes as she is surprised to see Callum holding her as he asks *"are you ok? You could have hurt yourself."* Gabriel says, *"rats my plan failed."* People are talking about Callum as they murmur *'how did he save her so fast? Did you see that?'*. Damien looks at Celeste and says, *"Callum come we need to talk."*

Chapter 16

As Damien and Callum go out to a side and walk; Damien says, *"I saw you saving Celeste."* Callum looks at Damien and attempts to do mind compulsion however Damien stops Callum and says, *"I know you are a vampire, don't worry I will keep your secret."* Callum thanks Damien as they shake hands. Callum looks around at the student as he closes his eyes and does a mind-wipe of the incident today. Damien opens his eyes as Callum says, *"you and only one other person knows what happened here?".* Damien sees Celeste as Callum says, *"she is not able to be compelled against my power."* One month passes in Cape town as it was starting to feel different; Celeste was glad to see Damien and Callum getting along however she still felt that Callum was hiding something, and he was mysterious. On the other side, Callum was getting closer to Celeste as he saw her sitting on the bench reading a book as he came to her and says *"hey Celly."* Celeste wasn't happy and says, *"what happened to Cel?".* Callum laughs and says, *"what's wrong with it? don't you like it?".* Celeste says, *"I prefer Cel please."* Callum nods as Celeste sees Callum is about to say something.

Callum says, *"there's somewhere I want to take you Cel."* Celeste asks *"where?".* Callum says, *"it's a surprise for tonight."* Damien saw Celeste and Callum as he wondered *'what are they up to?'.* As Callum leaves Celeste to continue studying; Damien comes over as Celeste says, *"hey".* Celeste thinks about Callum's surprise *'what's Callum up to? It better not be a date.'* Back at the castle, Carmilla was getting anxious as it had been over a month since Samara came with news regarding the DNA sample as Carmilla thought *'is it something bad? Is my son in danger?'.* As Celeste ate lunch with Damien; Damien asked, *"what are you doing this evening?".* Celeste wonders if Damien is asking her out as Celeste replies *"I have plans for tonight."* Damien looks a little sad however smiles and says, *"no worries."*

Back in the witches' hut, Samara had been working on the DNA result as she finally got what she had been waiting for as she had the document it showed what Celeste was. As Gabriel came in; Samara was looking at the document as she said, " *how was college sweetie?*". Gabriel then let out a huge, big burp that made the whole room shake like a mini earthquake. Samara looked angrily at Gabriel as Gabriel says, *"sorry I had a big bean burrito."* Samara grabs her wand as she began to zap Gabriel and says, " *you are a disgusting boy! burping in my room which is full of potions!*". Gabriel headed upstairs and locked his room as Samara says, *"you will not be getting dinner today!"*. Samara held the document and said, " *I have the document in my hand and tomorrow Carmilla will know the truth."*

Chapter 17

Later that evening Celeste was in town waiting for Callum as she thought *'he hasn't ditched me, has he?'*. Just then Callum came in casual clothes as Celeste says " *hey*". Callum says, *"come with me."* Callum takes Celeste's hands as they go through the forest as Celeste says, *"you brought me here to explore nature."* As Callum passes through a small cave; Celeste is curious as she goes through the cave and soon sees she is standing on a cliff as she turns to Callum she is about to slip as Callum holds her hand as she looks at him. Callum says, *"I've got you."* Celeste and Callum share an eye lock as Callum invites her to the blanket as they lay on it, looking at the night sky; Celeste says, *"this is nice and peaceful."* Callum says, *" don't close your eyes or you will miss the surprise."* Just the sky changes color as the stars come out and a meteor shower falls above the sky; Celeste laughs and smiles as she says, *"this is so beautiful."* Celeste turns to see Callum looking at her as she asks,*" don't you want to watch the stars?"*. Callum replies, *" I have my star in front of me."* Celeste blushes as she comes closer to Callum; just as their lips are about to touch; Celeste's phone rings as she sees it is Susie. Celeste says, *" I've got to go."* Callum helps her through the cave back as he says *" Cel I have something prepared for this weekend if you want."* Celeste nods as Callum drops her home.

The next day at college, Damien was talking with Celeste about the homework as Celeste was still in thoughts over Callum and their moment last night. Damien waves his hand and says, *"earth to Celeste."* Celeste apologizes as the bell rings for class; as Celeste comes in, she sees Callum sitting next to her seat as Celeste smiles at him; The teacher Mr. Gibson comes in with a student, a girl with long black wavy hair and brown eyes wearing a red casual dress. Mr. Gibson says, *"I want you to all meet Hannah our new student."* Hannah comes over to Celeste's seat as she says, *" I want to sit here."* Damien says, *" that's Celeste's seat."* As Hannah rolls her eyes; she says to Callum; *" Hi I'm Hannah."* As some of the guys approached Hannah. Callum thinks '*why are guys so stupid nowadays, before I became a vampire, I was not like this?*' After morning classes, Callum went to the library with Celeste and Damien as Hannah came there and sat at the table. Callum had his book over his face as he smelt a familiar scent as Hannah left before Callum could sense the smell deeper. Celeste asks, "*what are you thinking about?*". Callum replied "*nothing*".

As afternoon classes came; Mr. Gibson told Callum and Hannah to stay after class as everyone left. Callum asks, "*sir why have you kept me behind?*". Mr. Gibson says, "*Callum, I want you to be the one to show Hannah around the college.*" Callum says, "*why can't someone else do it, sir?*". Mr. Gibson gives him a death stare as Callum sighs and says, "*fine I will show her around sir.*" Hannah and Callum leave as Callum says, *I am going to see my friends.*" Hannah tags along as Celeste and Damien are waiting for him in the canteen. Celeste says "*Callum, Hannah's behind you.*" Hannah says "*I think we got off on a bad start. Let's start again; I'm Hannah.*" Celeste shakes her hand as does Damien.

Chapter 18

As Hannah holds Callum's arm excitedly, she says *"take me on a tour around the college."* As they leave; Celeste looks at them angrily as Damien asks, *"are you ok?"*. Celeste rolls her eyes as she takes her tray and leaves; Damien wonders *'is Celeste jealous?'*. As Celeste follows Callum quietly and observes Hannah. Damien taps her shoulder and says, *"are you spying on them?"*. Celeste shakes her head as Damien says, *"you have no reason to worry."* The next day Callum avoided Hannah as he says Celeste and said, *"I'm begging you... please save me."* Hannah comes as Callum runs away as Celeste says, *"Hannah why don't we have a talk?"*. As they walk down the corridor; Hannah says, *"you're so lucky to have a boyfriend like Callum."* Celeste says, *"Callum is not my boyfriend."* As Hannah laughs and chats with Celeste; Celeste thinks *'now I understand why Callum asked me to save him.'* Meanwhile, Carmilla was studying with Elise as the doorbell rings and the servant says, *"Your highness, Samara is here to see you."* As Carmilla says *"take a break Elise sweetie."* Carmilla says *"how is everything?"*. Samara hands the document to Carmilla who is stunned to see what Celeste is. Carmilla wonders and asks, *"could my son be in danger?"*. Samara says *"no she is special. This girl cannot be touched or harmed."* Carmilla was surprised and stunned as she thought *'could it be that the girl could also be my son's mate?'*.

As Samara leaves, she smirks and thinks *'I have put in the mind of Carmilla seeds of doubts.'* As she comes home; Gabriel sees his mom coming in and asks, *"where were you?"*. Samara replies *"on a mission sweetie."*. Later on, that evening Callum came to the kitchen and prepared a snack as Carmilla came in almost making Callum drop his sandwich. Carmilla says *"what's wrong son?"*. Callum replies *"mom you scared me."* Carmilla says *"well at least I can't scare you to death as we are undead."* Carmilla laughs and heads out as Callum sighs. Carmilla says *"I've got to find a way to talk to Celeste."* Meanwhile Hannah is in the

34

diner eating dinner as Damien comes and sees Hannah eating. Hannah says, *"hi Damien."*

Damien tries to avoid Hannah as Hannah says, *"fine just pretend I don't exist."* Damien then comes back as he sits with Hannah as she wipes a tear. Damien asks, *"what are you doing here this late?".* Hannah talks with Damien and says, *"I'll let you in on a secret; I am homeless."* Damien says, *"you can stay at my place if you want."* Hannah says, *"I don't want to be a burden."* Damien insists and brings her home as Hannah stays in the guest room; Hannah looks in the mirror at her reflection as she smiles evilly and thinks *'I will be able to complete my mission in being closer to Celeste and Callum.'*

Chapter 19

The next day Hannah awakes as she looks at the time as she makes a spell and disappears. As she comes home; Gabriel says, *"mom where were you this time?"*. Samara rolls her eyes as she heads inside as Gabriel leaves for college; Samara comes back into her room as she prepares the potions and drinks it. Damien comes to the guest room to check on Hannah and is surprised to see the room is empty. As Celeste and Callum come to the college; Damien is getting a snack as he sees them and says *"hey"*. Damien pays for the two-sausage roll and leaves as Hannah comes into the college wearing a different outfit as Damien says, *"Hannah where were you? here this is for you."* Hannah kisses Damien's cheek as they sit on the bench as Celeste and Callum watch them and say, *"do you think they are together?"*. Gabriel is walking down the corridor thinking about his mom as he bumps into Celeste. Callum holds his collar and says, *"can't you see where you are walking?"*. Gabriel apologizes and runs away as Celeste says, *"you need to learn to control your temper."* Callum rolls his eyes as the bell rings for class. Hannah sits next to Callum as Celeste sits next to Damien. As Hannah fawns over Callum as Damien says *"don't worry about Hannah. She's just like that."* At lunchtime, Callum and Celeste were eating as Damien and Hannah were sitting together. Callum says, *"this is weird, like how are Hannah and Damien friends."*

Celeste rolls her eyes and says, *"Callum don't tell me you like her."* Callum replies, *"no."* Celeste smiles hearing this as Callum says *"Cel what's your plan for this weekend?"*. Celeste says, *"I have nothing planned for this weekend."* Callum says, *"wrong you're spending it with me."* As Celeste finishes her homework; she heads home as Susie says *"there you are Celeste. It feels like I haven't seen you forever."* Celeste says, *"sorry sis I have been busy with school and..."* Susie says, *"let me guess Sexy man."* Celeste says, *"really Susie?"*. Susie says, *"I want to go out clubbing."* Celeste says, *"I am not going to drink."* Celeste gets changes as Susie finishes her makeup and then they leave. Celeste spots Hannah at the diner eating as Susie pulls her and says, *"come one slowpoke."* As Celeste comes back to the diner window it is empty as Celeste thinks *'could I have imagined Hannah was there?'*. As Hannah pops back from behind the wall she sighs and thinks *'that was close'*. Damien comes to the diner and sees Hannah and brings her home. Damien says, *"Hannah you can stay with me and eat too."* Hannah says, *"aww Damien you are so sweet."* Damien smiles as Hannah goes for a shower as she comes out with a towel around her and water dripping; Damien says, *"Hannah, I will get you another towel."* Hannah is about to slip as Damien holds her as they look into each other's eyes. Hannah thinks *'it's so easy to manipulate this fool. I can sense he is hiding a deep secret.'* Hannah chants a spell in her mind as Damien kisses Hannah as she pushes him off. Damien comes back to reality as Hannah pretends to be sad as she says, *"I can't believe you would try to take advantage of me."*

She runs to her room as Hannah has an evil smirk. Damien tries to remember what had happened as he cleans the bathroom and then heads downstairs to make dinner. Susie is dancing away as Celeste is at a table as Celeste feels tired; she sees Susie drunk as Celeste carries Susie home as Susie talks drunk *'I miss mom and Brianna.'* Later that evening Celeste comes to Brianna's grave and talks with her sister. Callum is passing as he sees her as he hears her thoughts which pain his heart. Callum thinks *' I hope our special weekend trip will bring a smile to your face.'* Friday came as Callum was excited for the weekend surprise as Celeste was busy with trying to get some of her assignments done. Hannah came over and said, *" Hey Celeste."* Celeste wondered and thought *' is now a good time to ask Hannah about what I saw last night?'*. Before Celeste could ask anything; Damien came and said, *"Hannah we need to talk."* Damien and Hannah come to a classroom as Damien apologizes for yesterday as Hannah pretends to act innocent and says, *" it was just a kiss, and it didn't mean anything."* As Callum passes by, he still is able to smell the scent and wonders, *'what does this smell remind me of?'.* Gabriel walks down the hall as sees Callum as he runs away. Callum laughs and says, *'he's frightened of me.'* Callum looks at the time and thinks *" only a few hours to go until my surprise for Cel."*

Chapter 20

As the day went by quickly; Celeste came home as she got changed and made sure everything was tidy. Susie had already left a note that she was out as Celeste came to Callum's place and rang the bell. Carmilla opens and sees Celeste as she says, *"hello dear, come in."* Celeste came inside as Carmilla said, *"Callum is almost ready; you can wait for him on the couch."* Celeste sits on the couch as she looks around as Callum comes down; they share a hug as Celeste says, *" Callum is this another one of your surprises?".* Callum asks, *"do you trust me?".* Celeste nods as he brings her to the park as Callum says, *" this is my favourite place in town."* Celeste smiles and says, *" it's so beautiful I can understand why you like this place."* They look at the sky as Isabelle walks in as she sees Callum and thought *' he's a vampire.'* As she tackles Callum to the ground; Celeste pushes her off and says, *"what the hell is wrong with you?".* Celeste asks, *"Callum are you ok?".* Callum says, *" I need some air alone please."* He walks down the path as Isabelle says, *"you're in danger he's a vampire."* Celeste laughs as she says, *"walk with me."*

Celeste and Isabelle walk as Isabelle introduces herself and says, *" I'm Isabelle, I am a Vampire hunter."* Celeste laughs again as she says, *" Vampires aren't real and don't exist."* Isabelle had a serious expression as Celeste saw as she stopped laughing. *"I'm Celeste by the way."* Isabelle frowned and said, *" I know Vampires are real, they killed my parents."* Celeste rolls her eyes and says, *" if they were real, I'm not saying there are not all are going to be evil."* Isabelle pushes Celeste and says, *"you'll never understand."* Meanwhile, Callum was on his walk as Darren came beside him as he says, *" oh my god you're covered in grass what happened?".* Callum looks up and sees a guy with red eyes just like him as he says, *"you're a vampire too."* Darren smiles and says, *" yeah my name is Darren, and you are?".*

Callum introduces himself and shakes Darren's hand as Darren asks *" Callum, how long have you been a vampire for?".* Callum replies *" a few years what about you?".* as Darren helps fix Callum's hair he replies, *"about a month now."* As they talked, Isabelle and Celeste came back as Isabelle sees Darren and says, *" Darren what are you doing out here? what if Gabriella or Danny tries to hurt you again."* Darren assures her as he says, *" I know how to protect myself Isabelle."* As Isabelle and Darren turn to leave, they wave goodbye to their new friends. Celeste links her arms into Callum as she asks, *" are you ok?".* Callum says, *" I will be now that you are here."*

Chapter 21

Callum and Celeste share a moment as he takes her home. The next day Samara is in her hut working on a potion as Gabriel comes in asking *"mom, what is up with you?"*. Samara replies, *"you don't ask me questions, Gabriel"*. Gabriel leaves for college as Samara takes a potion with her. Celeste comes to the college early as she decides to practice on the field. Hannah comes out on the field as Celeste says, *" hi Hannah, how are you?"*. Hannah says, *" I want to practice, show me"*. After observing Celeste's moves, Hannah asks, *" wanna play a match?"*. Celeste replies, *"sure"*. Hannah and Celeste play against each other as their game attracts a small crowd student who cheers for both. Hannah's eyes change for a minute as she thinks *'time to end the game'*. Hannah scores the final goal as Celeste catches her breath for a minute. Hannah extends her hand as she says, *" it was a good game"*. Damien comes out onto the field as he sees Hannah and says, *"hey Hannah"*. Hannah goes with Damien as Celeste grabs a bottle of water. Callum comes out on the field as he sees Celeste and says *" hey Cel"*.

Celeste turns to Callum as she says, *"hey Callum"*. The bell rings as Celeste heads for a shower as Callum waits for Celeste in class. Back in the castle, Carmilla was teaching Elise as Elise asks Carmilla a question about her powers. Elise notices Carmilla is in deep thoughts as she shakes her mom asking, *" is everything, ok mama?"*. Carmilla nods as she says, *"Elise sweetie, why don't you go do training with your dad?"*. Elise happily goes as Carmilla thinks to speak to Samara about Celeste. Hannah is in class with Damien as Callum comes in with Celeste. Hannah says, *" we played a great game out there Celeste"*. Carmilla takes a trip to Samara's hut as Hannah's bracelet gives her a shock. She raises her hand to leave as she comes out into the corridor and checks that Carmilla is outside her hut. Hannah sighs and thinks *'I will need to find a way to get rid of her soon.'* Hannah does a spell as she teleports back into her hut and changes back into Samara. Carmilla knocks on the door as Samara opens and says, *"your majesty what are you doing here?"*.

Carmilla comes in as she tries to know more about Celeste's truth however Samara says, *"I have only told you what I know"*. Samara sighs and says, *"I have work to attend to and I am sure you also have things to do"*. Samara walks Carmilla out as she thinks *'why is Samara acting strange? It's like she is up to something'.* Carmilla heads back to the castle; meanwhile, back at the college it was lunchtime as Celeste and Callum sat together as Callum says, *"this weekend didn't go as planned"*. Celeste smiles and says, *"it was nice, and I made a new friend"*. Celeste wondered *'should I mention to* Callum *what Isabelle had told me?'.* Celeste and Callum ate as Damien came and asked, *"have you guys seen Hannah?"*. Hannah comes into the canteen as she apologizes for leaving earlier. Celeste's phone rings as she sees an incoming call from Susie. She heads out to take the call as Susie says *"hey Cel, you wouldn't believe who got the last VIP ticket for Wolf Club"*. Celeste says, *"you know I don't really do clubbing and partying"*. Susie says, *"come on Celeste, you are my sister, and you are supposed to be on my side"*.

Celeste sighs and says, *"fine I will come with you"*. Susie says, *"it's for tomorrow night"*. Susie ends the call as she heads out to do some shopping. Callum comes behind Celeste as she feels a little spooked and says, *"Callum, can you not sneak up on me?"*. Callum apologizes as he asks, *"Is everything ok?"*. Celeste sees Gabriel looking at her as she goes over to him replying, *"what is your problem, Gabriel? what do you want?"*. Gabriel laughs and says, *"Callum's not who you think he is!"*. Gabriel corners Celeste against the locker as he tries to flirt with her. However, the next thing which happens is Callum punching Gabriel and warns him to stay away from Celeste. Hannah sees Callum beating Gabriel as Hannah clenches her fist and thinks *'I will make Callum pay for beating my son'.*

Chapter 22

C eleste comes in between Callum and Gabriel as she says "*Callum, stop it please*". The teacher comes and says, "*what on earth is going on here?*". Callum broodily walks away as Celeste apologizes to the teacher for the disturbance. Gabriel looks at Celeste and says, "*why did you come between us?*". Celeste sighs as she says, "*I am not interested in your fights so please just stay away from me and Callum*". Celeste leaves as Hannah comes over to Gabriel and she asks, "*are you ok?*". Gabriel nods as he leaves leaving Hannah in thoughts. Callum comes to the castle as he heads to his room thinking about the fight. He punches a wall in anger and thinks '*anyone who tries to hurt Celeste or play her I will always fight for her.*' There is a knock on his bedroom door as Callum says, "*come in*".

Carmilla comes in with a glass of juice as she asks, "*how was your day at school Callum?*". Carmilla sees a scratch on Callum's hand as it soon heals. Carmilla says, "*how many times have me, and your dad told you not to get into fights?*". Callum says coldly "*this guy was bothering Celeste and if anyone hurts her or anything I won't spare them*". His eyes change red as Carmilla calms him down. He drinks the juice as Carmilla thinks '*Callum is very protective over this human girl*'. Callum notices Carmilla in deep thought as he asks, "*mom are you ok?*". Carmilla nods as she says, "*it's fine I was going to talk to you about something, but it can wait*". Later that afternoon as Celeste comes home; Elijah is drinking a bottle of alcohol as he says drunk "*look who decided to show up*". Celeste says, "*dad have you got nothing better to do than drink stupid!*". Elijah argues with Celeste as she heads up to her room. Susie comes downstairs as Elijah says, "*your sister is a silly girl!*". Susie knocks on Celeste's door as she opens it to find Celeste laying on her bed crying. Susie comforts her sister as Celeste says, "*dad is the worst, and I don't know how you put up with him*". Susie asks, "*how about we do something together? Let's go shopping*".

Susie and Celeste come to the mall as the lady from the spa sees Susie again asking, *"Susie, what a nice surprise to see you back!"*. Susie says, *"can I get the facial treatment for my sister?"*. Celeste gets a relaxing facial done as Susie soon treats her for dinner. Celeste eats a burger as she says, *" thanks sis, I really need this today"*. Back at the castle, Vlad was feeling restless as he wanted to go and hunt. He opened Callum's room as Callum says, *"dad what are you doing in my room?"*. Vlad asks, *"son, would you like to join me on a hunt?"*. Callum nods as he puts his shoes on; Susie and Celeste walk home as Elijah is passed out drunk on the couch. Susie feels full after the big dinner as she says, *" I am going for a run"*. Celeste sits on the chair as she says, *"do I have to?"*. Susie and Celeste get changed as Celeste grabs a water bottle and they both take a run into the woods. Susie and Celeste both enjoy the cold breeze as Celeste takes a shortcut as Susie looks around the woods calling her name. Vlad and Callum are both above the trees as they look for a human to feast on. Celeste keeps running when she suddenly trips over a branch and cuts her arm. Celeste says *"ouch, this is so painful"*. Callum's eyes change red as he leaves Vlad as Vlad sees Susie and thinks *' she will make a perfect feast'*. Vlad corners Susie as she turns around and yells *"WHO IS THERE? SHOW YOURSELF!"*.

Vlad is about to feed on Susie as she grabs a wooden log and hits Vlad as she runs away. Vlad hisses angrily as Celeste slowly walks down the path she is stunned when she passes the cemetery. Callum comes to the smell of blood as Celeste walks into the cemetery followed by Callum behind her. Celeste feels a shadow behind her as she turns and sees Callum. Celeste asks, *" Callum, what are you doing here so late?"*. Callum sees her wound as he rips a piece of his shirt and ties it around Celeste. Callum hugs Celeste as his eyes flicker between his normal eyes and vampire's eyes. Callum thinks *' I need to control myself and I am not going to hurt Celeste'*. Celeste brings Callum over to Brianna's grave as she says, *"every day I miss her more."* Callum holds Celeste's hand as she smiles at him. Susie soon comes home calling for Celeste however no response; Susie wonders *' what if Celeste ran into the monster in the woods?'.* Back in Samara's hideout, she was busy concocting a potion as she pours a green liquid into a vial and thinks *' this will be the best way to get back at you Callum'.* She laughs evilly as Gabriel comes and says *" mom, it's late can I please sleep in peace?".* Samara rolls her eyes as Gabriel heads upstairs to sleep.

Chapter 23

The next morning Celeste comes home as Susie runs and hugs her. Susie asks, *"are you ok?"*. Susie sees the cloth wrapped around her arm as Susie opens it to show a small cut; Susie brings the first aid box and does her dressing. Celeste's phone beeps as she sees a message from Callum which makes her smile. Later, Celeste comes to college as Damien sees the bandage on her arm as he asks, *" are you ok? how did you get hurt?"*. Celeste says, *"running yesterday, but I'm fine"*. Hannah comes there as she gives Damien and Celeste a sports drink as Callum walks down the corridor and Hannah smiles and says, *"this is for you!"*. Callum is about to reject it as he notices Celeste watching him as he takes it from her happily. Hannah smiles as she walks away; Celeste and Damien look at the bottle as Damien throws it in the bin and Celeste says, *"I will take it to my sister"*.

As they all head to class; Callum is about to throw the drink away as Hannah's magic stops him as Callum says, *"I guess I will be drinking you later"*. Back at the castle, Vlad was feeling angry as he wasn't able to feed or hunt. Carmilla comes with a bottle of blood as Vlad says *"why does it feel like I am losing my touch? the humans are the weaklings"*. Carmilla pours a glass of blood as Vlad drinks it. Carmilla says, *"don't worry my love, I know you will get your hunt soon"*. Later that afternoon Hannah watches and sneaks to make sure Callum drinks the juice; Callum takes it out of his bag as he opens it and drinks it. Hannah smirks as Gabriel taps her shoulder and asks, *"um Hannah, are you ok?"*. Hannah straightens up as she smiles and nods before walking away. Later that afternoon in class; Callum begins to act weird as he touches Celeste's hand and plays with her hair. Celeste says *"Callum, please stop acting strangely"*. After class in the corridor, Callum pulls Celeste and spins her in his arm as she tries to push him off however Callum pulls her closer and forcibly kisses her. Damien comes in between as he pushes Callum off her. Damien says, *"she already told you to leave her alone!"*. Celeste cries as she pulls her silver necklace and throws it at Callum.

She runs off as Callum looks around as the room spins in his mind; Celeste comes home as she remembers Callum behaving strangely. Celeste thinks '*why is acting like this?*'. Susie comes down as she sees Celeste's sad face and asks *"sis, is everything ok?"*. Celeste tells Susie about Callum's behaviour as Susie says,*" I can't believe Sexyman forced you to dance and kiss!"*. Celeste rolls her eyes as she says,*" are we still up for going to the party tonight?"*. That evening Celeste dresses up with Susie as they head to the Wolf Pack club and party the night. Vlad is in the woods hunting as he says, *"no matter what happens, I will hunt my prey"*. Damien is at the club as he sees Celeste and asks, *"how are you feeling?"*. Celeste sighs and replies *" thanks for helping me but I can't imagine why Callum was acting up today"*. Elsewhere, Callum is at home as he has the silver necklace as he thinks *' why is my head pounding? what's happening to me?'*. Callum calls his mom as he collapses on the floor; Carmilla brings a bottle of blood as she tries to wake him up. Celeste and Damien share a dance as Susie gets drunk. Susie notices Damien and Celeste as she comes over and introduces herself; Celeste holds Susie as Susie says, *" I am fine, you need to loosen up sis!"*. Celeste asks, *" Damien do you have a car?"*. Damien nods as Celeste asks, *" I need to take my sister home, she's drunk and the wood route is just too long"*. Damien asks, *"how about I take you both home safely?"*. Susie grabs another drink as she stumbles outside the door; She begins to walk into the forest laughing and too drunk. Vlad watches her from the trees and thinks '*this time there will be no escape for you.* His eyes change red as he pounces down from the tree.

Chapter 24

Celeste thanks Damien as she goes to look for Susie; outside in the woods Vlad is feeding off Susie as she struggles to get free. Celeste comes out as Susie screams when Vlad drops her and leaves; Celeste says, *"that scream sounded like Susie"*. Back at the castle, Callum was feeling a lot better as he says, *"mom thanks for helping me"*. Carmilla smiles as Callum soon gets a feeling and leaves unexpectedly. Celeste and Damien search the woods for Susie; meanwhile, Callum runs through the woods as he sees Vlad feeding off Susie and stopping his dad. Vlad says, *"how dare you to stop me, son!"*. Callum says *"what are you going to do? Kill her?"*. Vlad leaves as he grabs another girl as she screams; Celeste says, *"it came from over there"*. As Celeste runs up a hill; she sees the dark shadow biting the girl as it growls at her and disappears. Damien sees the young girl who drops dead as Celeste covers her mouth in shock. Celeste says, *"this girl is around the same age as Brianna"*. Celeste takes off her jacket as she covers the girl as Celeste says to Damien *"we need to find my sister"*. Callum held Susie as he tried to find a pulse however it was very weak; Callum bit his wrist and tried to feed her his blood as he soon heard Celeste's voice. Celeste called out *"SUSIE! SUSIE!"*. Celeste soon sees something in the foggy mist as she walks into it and sees Callum beside Susie; Celeste says, *"Callum what are you doing here?"*. Celeste sees Susie on the floor unconscious with a mark around her neck as Celeste bends down and says *"sis, wake up!"*.

Damien is shocked as Celeste says, *"we need to get her to a hospital"*. As Damien drives Susie to the hospital, Celeste prays for her sister as Callum tries to comfort her however Celeste says, *"I think you hurt my sister"*. Callum was shocked as he says, *"why would I do that?"*. As Celeste waits anxiously outside; back in the woods the police have been searching for clues as all they have is blood; The police officers come to the hospital to get some answers as Celeste says, *"I think Callum know more about what is happening"*. The officer takes Callum in for questioning as Celeste waits for news on Susie. Damien comes with a coffee as Celeste says, " *I can't lose her, I lost Brianna a few months ago*". She cries as Damien assures her everything will be ok. Celeste tries to get some sleep as she remembers seeing the figure with fangs as she dreams about Callum being the monster who killed Susie and is about to attack her. Celeste wakes up as she breathes rapidly as she looks around to see she is safe; she sees the doctor and asks *"doctor, how is my sister doing?"*. The doctor replies *" I am sorry, but she is still very critical"*.

Celeste waits outside as Damien gets a call from Hannah. Hannah asks, *"Damien where are you?"*. Damien replies *" I just had a personal emergency"*. Hannah tells Damien to come soon as Damien turns to Celeste and asks, *" will you be, ok?"*. Celeste nods as she thanks Damien for helping her today. Back at the castle, Vlad comes home angrily as Carmilla asks " *my love, what has gotten you so angry?"*. Vlad says " *our son wanted me to stop feeding on a breather! So, we have killed many humans"*. Callum comes into the room as he says, " *you were feeding on Celeste's sister"*. Vlad says, " *you never seemed to be catching feelings before of humans"*. Callum's eyes changes to red in anger as he challenges Vlad to a duel. Callum says, *" If I win, you are to leave the humans alone forever"*. Vlad growls as his eyes change and ask, " *what about if I win and you lose?"*. Vlad says, *" let's make it interesting, if I win, I feed on the human girl Celeste"*. Callum clenches his fist in anger and thinks *'I will never let you harm Celeste'*. Back in the hospital, Celeste had finished her 8th cup of coffee as she thought of her dream and wondered ' *is Callum really a blood-sucking monster?'*.

Chapter 25

Celeste thinks *'maybe I am just thinking too much.'* A nurse sees Celeste waiting as she says *"dear, you can go home."* Celeste says, *" I can't leave my sister, what if something happens".* The nurse assures that Susie is in safe hands as Celeste heads home; she sees her dad passed out drunk on the sofa as she climbs upstairs and soon falls asleep. Back at the castle Vlad and Callum were preparing to duel as Carmilla says *" stop this nonsense, both of you!".* Vlad says *" I will not back out of this! I am the King and the most powerful Vampire".* Callum says, *"your time will be over old man and I will win!".* Vlad's eyes change red as Callum's eyes change too as they begin to fight and use their powers; Carmilla watches from a corner as Vlad is winning at first however Callum thinks of Celeste and remembers Susie as he manages to push Vlad to the corner.

Callum sees Vlad feeling weak and out of breath as holds his hand and says *"you win boy! I won't feed on humans".* Callum says *" just your word is not enough dad! I need your signature!".* Callum brings out a contract as Vlad sees it and says, *" what is this? are you siding with the humans?".* Callum says, *" Humans and Vampires can co-exist peacefully".* Vlad rolls his eyes as he signs it and says,*" no fun!".* Vlad soon heads to his coffin with Carmilla as Callum smiles seeing the contract. The next day Celeste comes to the hospital early to see Susie as she is shocked to see Callum sitting beside her sister. Callum says in a friendly tone, *"hi Celeste".* Celeste ignores him as Susie opens her eyes and takes a deep breath as she turns to see Callum and says *" hello sexyman!".* Celeste says *" Susie, how are you feeling?".* Susie winces as she feels a bandage around her neck as she replies *" how did I get here? I don't remember what happened".*

Callum tries to calm Susie down as Celeste gives Callum a cold look as Callum wonders *'why is Celeste acting so frosty towards me?'.* Celeste says, *" I have to get to college, but I will see you in the evening".*

Celeste grabs her bag as Callum goes after Celeste and says " *Celeste, why are you ignoring me? what have I done?"*. Celeste remembers the dream as she backs away from Callum and she replies *" look, I have things to do ok. please just leave me alone".* Callum is hurt by Celeste's behaviour as she comes to the college and sees Damien. Damien notices Celeste has had a rough night as Celeste says "*Damien, can we go talk somewhere private please?".* Meanwhile, at the castle Vlad is in a deep sleep as Carmilla heads out to meet Samara; Samara is brewing a potion as Carmilla comes in and says, *"I need your help".* Samara makes a pot of tea as Carmilla tells Samara what happened last night.

Samara thinks evilly *'already father and son are fighting'.* Carmilla cries as Samara tries to comfort her and gives her two potions; Carmilla asks *"what will they do?".* Samara says,*" they will help ease pain and suffering".* Carmilla soon leaves as Samara smirks; Gabriel comes downstairs and asks, " *what was she doing here?".* Samara says, *"don't you have anything better to do than spy on me son?".* Gabriel rolls his eyes as he heads back upstairs. Samara thinks ' *if she does as I told her, then by tomorrow night the Queen will be dead'.* Back in the college, Celeste is sitting in the canteen as Damien brings over two hot chocolates as he says "*Celeste, how is Susie doing now?".* Celeste breaks down as she tells Damien how she is feeling however she doesn't mention her dream. Damien gives her a hug as Callum comes into the canteen and sees Susie and Damien close as he clenches his fist in anger.

Chapter 26

Callum comes over to Celeste and Damien as he says, "*hey guys*". Celeste feels uncomfortable as she gets up to leave however Callum sarcastically says " *Celeste, are you ok? I didn't mean to interrupt your date*". Celeste rolls her eyes and leaves as Damien asks, "*Callum bro, are you ok?*". Callum throws Damien to the corner as he warns Damien to stay away from Celeste. Meanwhile, at the hospital, Susie wakes up as she gets up and removes the bandage from her neck to see the bite mark in the mirror. Susie screams as her reflections fade in and out. The nurse comes inside to see Susie without her bandage as Susie screams *"what happened to me?"*. Susie struggles to contain herself as the nurse calls the doctor who sedates her; the nurse looks at the doctor and asks, " *will she be, ok?*". The doctor says, " *her wound indicates that a wild beast has tried to kill her*".

Elsewhere, Celeste comes to a café as she orders coffee when someone comes in and says, *"make those two coffees"*. Celeste recognizes the voice as she turns to see Isabelle. Isabelle smiles and says, " *hi Celeste, how have you been?*". Celeste and Isabelle grab a table as Celeste replies " *I'm fine Isabelle, how are you?*". Isabelle is a little shaken as Celeste places her hand on hers and asks " *Isabelle, you're shaking*". Isabelle tells Celeste about Darren's truth as Celeste is stunned. Isabelle says, " *it still doesn't feel real, I can't believe that he's a Vampire*". As their coffee arrives; they both drink it as Isabelle asks, " *I was wondering, what made you call me?*". Celeste doesn't know how to start the conversation as she says, *"Vampires are real??"*. Isabelle sighs as she looks at Celeste and says, " *the last time we met; you didn't think they existed*". Celeste drinks a sip of coffee as she says " *Isabelle, I had a strange dream last night that Callum was a Vampire*". Isabelle says, "*sometimes our dreams can become real and other times it might just be a nightmare*". Celeste says, " *it's too hard to know what is real and what is not.*" Isabelle gives Celeste some advice on how to spot a Vampire as she gives Celeste a stake as Celeste asks *"a wooden stake! I thought you would have gotten me some garlic?"*. Isabelle rolls her eyes and says, *"look if you think Callum is a threat, Vampires die by a stake to the heart"*. Celeste examines it as she asks, *"how do you know all these things?"*. Isabelle becomes emotional for a moment and mentions her parents as Celeste tells her about her mother. Isabelle hugs Celeste as she says, *" if you need to talk again, you have my number ok!"*. Celeste waves goodbye as Isabelle leaves.

Meanwhile, back in the castle, Carmilla prepares two drinks as she serves one to Vlad as Callum comes and says *"mom, can I have one?"*. Carmilla shakes her head as Callum brings her to the living room to sit. Carmilla says *"Callum, I need to take the drink up to your dad"*. Callum asks *"mom, are you mad at me? for winning the duel and stopping the feed on humans?"*. Carmilla replies *" I am not mad with you; it's just feeding on humans who have been our ways for centuries"*. Callum says, *"although it hasn't been long living as a vampire, I was a human once"*. Callum asks, *"do you love me any less?"*. Carmilla has blood tears running from her eyes as she hugs Callum and says *" don't you ever say this again! I love you and Elise equally."* Callum says *" I love you too mom"*; later that evening in the hospital, Susie awakes as she feels a strong smell coming from nearby as she follows it. She sees a small blood bank as she feels hunger; Susie sees a guy handling the blood as Susie says, *"you come here!"*. Susie's eyes turn red for a moment as the guy walks away as Susie jumps over the counter and grabs a blood bag. She opens it and licks it as she feels her hunger being satisfied. Susie soon feels weak as she collapses as the nurses find her and bring her to her room; the doctor tries to call Celeste and Celeste picks up and hears about Susie. Celeste says worriedly, *" I am coming"*.

Chapter 27

As Celeste rushes over to the hospital, she comes into Susie's room as she is shocked to see the bed empty and a nurse in the corner unconscious with a bite mark on her neck. Celeste bends over as she taps on the nurse who opens her red eyes and hisses at Celeste. Celeste stakes her heart as the nurse turns to dust; Celeste says, *"I am so sorry"*. she wipes a tear away as the doctor comes in to see Celeste and says, *" we need to talk about your sister"*. Celeste asks *" what happened? Where is Susie?"*. Meanwhile, back at the castle, Vlad was in his room training his powers as Carmilla says *"sweetheart, I have made a special drink for you"*. Vlad rolls his eyes as he asks, *"if it's not blood, I do not want it"*. Carmilla adds a few drops of blood as Vladimir drinks it and soon falls asleep. Carmilla drinks the other juice as she decides to head out. Back at the hospital, Celeste is shocked after hearing Susie has been ripping and killing people like a monster. Celeste says *" no, my sister is not some kind of blood-sucking monster"*. Celeste decides to call Susie however there is no response. Celeste vows to find her sister; back in the town, Susie is killing everyone as Callum spots her. Susie flashes her red eyes at Callum as he shows her his eyes, and says *"Susie, you need to calm down and stop killing everyone"*. Susie calms down for a moment as she says *"sexyman, you are also like me with red eyes"*.

Callum says, *" I am a Vampire and not an ordinary one"*. Callum says, *"let's go talk somewhere else"*. Celeste comes home as she sees her dad still sleeping on the couch however he has no neck bite or mark. Celeste thinks *'Susie hasn't come home, where could she be?'*. Susie and Callum are at a hilltop as Callum tries to control Susie and says, *" I know you have a huge urge to feed yourself, but you killing everyone puts the Vampires at risk"*. Susie looks at Callum as she says, *" my life really is over; I can't go back to college or have a normal life"*. Callum tries to comfort her as she kisses him however Callum stops and says *"Susie, I like you but only as a friend and I am sure you will find your mate soon"*. Susie is embarrassed as Callum says, *" I am going to call your sister to come to pick you up."* As Callum turns to make a call; Susie smells a strong smell coming from the woods as she goes after it. Celeste calls Damien as he asks *"Celeste, is everything ok?"*. Celeste says *"no, something has happened to Susie"*. As Carmilla walks in the woods; she feels her head becoming heavy and wonders *'what is happening to me?'*. Elsewhere, Samara is watching Carmilla's suffer through a cauldron and thinks *'your time is almost up.* Celeste comes into the woods as Susie sees Carmilla. Carmilla asks *"I need some help!"*. Susie's eyes change to red as she bits Carmilla's neck. Carmilla screams as Celeste runs in the direction. Celeste sees Susie feeding on Carmilla as she screams *"SUSIE STOP!"*. Susie growls at her as Celeste shows the stake and warns her *"get back or I will stake you!"*. Susie flees as Celeste comes over to Carmilla as Carmilla looks at Celeste and says weakly, *"you are Callum's.."*; Celeste replies *" his friend.. I am going to get some help for you"*. Carmilla says *" I feel my end is near, promise me you will take care of Callum"*. Celeste tries to comfort her as her phone rings; Celeste sees Callum's call as she picks up. Callum asks *" Celeste, where are you? we need to talk"*. Celeste has tears in her eyes as she says *" Callum, please come to the forest right now!"*.

As Carmilla begins to feel weaker; she pulls Celeste closer and whispers something in her ear before dying. Callum comes to the wood as he is shocked to see his mother lying on the floor dead. Callum has tears in his eyes and says *"mom, wake up!"*. As Celeste gets up, a wooden stake drops out of her bag as Callum looks at Celeste with anger and hate. Celeste says *"Callum, I know who did this to your mom"*. Callum gets angry as he says *"you killed my mom! I will never forgive you for this!"*. Celeste attempts to explain however Callum uses his superstrength and throws her against a tree as she falls unconscious. Callum strokes his mother's forehead and carries her back to the castle. Back at Samara's hut, Samara laughs evilly as she says, *"so Callum hates*

Celeste? the plan is working a treat". She pours herself a glass of bubbly and celebrates Carmilla's death.

Chapter 28

The next day as the sun rises, Callum is in the living room with Carmilla as he cries; Vlad comes down with Elise as Vlad sees Carmilla laying on the floor. He covers Elise's eyes as he bows down to Carmilla and says *"my love, wake up! Speak to me"*. Callum looks at Vlad as he says, *"mom's dead... Celeste killed her"*. Vlad's eyes change to dark red as he says, *"I will kill that girl!"*. Callum stops Vlad as he says, *"I will deal with her, we need to make preparations for mom's funeral"*. Back in the woods, Celeste is unconscious as a little girl sees her as she says *"daddy, look there's a girl hurt"*. Celeste is brought to the hospital; meanwhile, Susie is hiding in the trees as she thinks *'what have I done?'*. The doctors call the last person on Celeste's phone as Callum picks up. He hears about Celeste's accident as he says, *"try someone who actually cares about her!"*. The doctor calls Damien who rushes over to the hospital; a few hours later Celeste opens her eyes as she sees Damien beside her and asks *"Damien, what are you doing here?"*. Damien takes Celeste's hand and says, *"thank god, someone found you and brought you here"*. Celeste asks about Callum as Damien says, *"I will call him"*. Damien calls Callum as he picks up; Damien says *"hey Callum, where are you? Celeste has..."*. Callum angrily says, *"I don't want to hear or know about Celeste"*. He ends the call as Celeste looks sadly at Damien as she begins to cry.

Damien tries to cheer her up as Susie comes to the door. Meanwhile, back at Samara's hut, she was busy celebrating as Gabriel asks *"mom, you have been acting so strange lately are you ok?"*. Samara says, *"our plan to take over the Vampire kingdom will work a treat; the Queen of the Vampires is dead"*. Gabriel is stunned and asks, *"mom, did you kill her?"*. Samara rolls her eyes as Gabriel says, *"I can't believe you could do something so wicked"*. Samara warns Gabriel not to get soft as Gabriel leaves for college. Back at the castle, Vlad is preparing Carmilla's funeral as Elise cries and says, *"I want to see my mommy"*.

Callum brings Elise to her room as she cries asking for Carmilla. Callum hugs Elise and says, "*we need to be brave for our mom sis*". Back at the hospital, Celeste is shocked to see Susie as Damien says, "*I will get some food*". Susie says, "*sis how are you feeling?*". Celeste says, "*don't call me that! what you did was wrong*. Susie feels remorseful as she says, "*I am sorry, I never meant to kill*".

Celeste slowly gets up as her head still hurts as Celeste says, "*after what you did, Callum hurt me and blames me for his mom's death*". Susie says, "*I will speak to sexyman*". Celeste warns Susie as Susie's darker Vampire side comes out as she says "*I am done begging, being a sad pathetic human. I will embrace my darker side and Celeste remember that you killed mother*". Celeste says, "*that is not true, I would never hurt mama*". Susie laughs coldly and says, "*I will find Brianna's killer*". Susie leaves as Celeste thinks '*it's for the best she leaves*'. Damien comes back with food as Celeste says, "*thanks Damien, you are such a great friend*". Elsewhere Vlad buries Carmilla with a few vampires as Callum thinks '*mom, I swear I will make Celeste pay for your death*'. Later that night as Celeste is asleep in the hospital, Callum sneaks into her room; he grabs Celeste by her neck as she awakes and sees Callum's red eyes as she chokes; Callum coldly says, "*I am going to make you feel death*". Celeste tries to say "Callum...*Cal..um*". Celeste manages to hit the emergency button as Callum leaves the room. Celeste catches her breath as the nurse asks, "*are you ok Celeste?*".

Chapter 29

Celeste takes a moment to catch her breath as she asks, "*can I have some water please?*". As the nurse gives her a glass to drink; Celeste thanks her and tries to rest however she begins to cry thinking that Callum hates her. As Callum comes back to the castle; Vlad asks, "*is the girl dead yet?*". Callum replies "*not yet dad, I will give her a slow and painful death.*" A few days pass by as Celeste soon leaves the hospital and comes home; Elijah sees her and drunkenly says "*so, you are still here and alive?*". Celeste ignores him as she goes upstairs and takes out a framed photo of her mom. She sits on the floor clutching the photo frame close to her chest and cries "*mom, I wish you were here with me*". Celeste closes her eyes for a moment as a gentle breeze blows on her face; she opens her eyes to see a white light and a ghost figure of her mom smiling at her. Celeste cries "*mom, I am sorry*". Amanda says "*sweetie, you are not to blame for what happened to me*". Celeste tries to touch her mom as Amanda says, "*I know you will find a way to make things work between you and Callum*". Celeste says "*mom, he's a Vampire*". Amanda says, "*when the heart falls in love, things like dead or alive, age or size doesn't matter*". Amanda says, "*I will always be with you*". Amanda wipes Celeste's tears as she soon leaves. Celeste opens her eyes and looks around the room however Amanda's spirit has already left. Celeste gets up as she says, "*I am going to be strong, and I won't let Callum break me!*".

Back at the witches' hut, Samara was concocting a potion as Gabriel came asking "*mom, what's your next plan?*". Samara smirks evilly "*I will attempt to manipulate and control Vladimir's mind*". Gabriel rolls his eyes as he says, "*I've got to get to class*". Samara watches Gabriel leaves and wonders '*why is my son so useless?*'. Back at college, Callum gave cold looks to Celeste as Damien came over to her asking "*is everything ok Celeste?*". Celeste shakes her head as she is about to cry as Damien looks around, and says "*Celeste, come with me?*". Damien brings Celeste into an empty classroom as pulls down the curtain and turns on the light. Damien says "*Celeste, I know you are trying to be strong about everything*". Celeste says " *Damien, when I first moved here with my family, I thought this was going to be a loving and safe village;*". Damien grabs a box of tissue as Celeste tells Damien about her sisters and mom. Damien asks, " *what about your dad?*". Celeste rolls her eyes as she says "*he's not a good father! He's an alcoholic and abusive*". Damien places a hand on Celeste assuring her that things will get better. Celeste cries" *how can I know that everything will be, ok? Susie is a blood-sucking monster, Brianna is dead, and Callum..*". She stops for a moment as Damien asks, "*what were you going to say about Callum?*". Celeste doesn't say anything as she comes out. Damien thinks '*I need to talk to Callum about this*'. Celeste comes to the changing room as she heads out on the field to practice. Callum comes as he says, "*how about we train together?*".

Callum uses his vampire powers to hurt Celeste kicking the ball at her until Celeste falls to the ground. Callum hovers above her with his red eyes as he says coldly, "every minute I will make your life difficult. "*I will give you death!*". Celeste cries as suddenly Callum hears footsteps and leaves; Damien comes over to Celeste and helps her up as he asks " *Celeste, you have just come out of the hospital. You should be resting not playing*". Celeste leans on Damien as she replies, " *I am fine*". Damien decides to treat Celeste for dinner as Susie follows and watches Celeste and thinks ' *I will make Sexyman mine*'. Later that night, Callum is training in his room when Susie climbs in and says "*hey Sexyman*". Callum rolls his eyes as he says, "*what do you want Susie?*". Susie says, "*you're the Vampire prince and surely you can help me out!*". Callum asks, "what's *in it for me?!*". Susie smirks evilly and says, "*I will help you in getting revenge and justice for your mom*". Callum pins Susie against the wall as Susie kisses Callum passionately. Callum lifts her still passionately kissing her as he takes her to the bed. Meanwhile, Celeste is at Damien's place as she looks out of the window at the sky. Damien gives Celeste a delicious lasagne with salad as Celeste takes a few bites. Damien says, *"you know, you can always stay with me if you need a place"*. Celeste thanks Damien wiping a tear from her eyes *"you're such a great friend, thanks for everything"*.

Chapter 30

The next morning Callum wakes up as he sees Susie in his shirt holding a bottle of blood. She smirks *"Good morning sexyman"*. Callum gets up as he says *"Susie, what are you doing here? last night..."*. Susie says, *"it was hot and magical"*. Susie tries to kiss Callum however Callum pushes her away saying *"last night was a mistake! I was angry and it shouldn't have happened."* Susie looks annoyed as she leaves; Callum wonders *'why does it feel like I have cheated Celeste?'*. Celeste and Damien come to school as Hannah calls out *"Damien, Celeste"*. Damien asks, *"hi Hannah, where have you been?"*. Hannah replies *"just dealing with some personal stuff. what have I missed?"*. Hannah sees Callum as she turns to Celeste asking, *"are you together now?"*. Celeste shakes her head as she heads to class on the way down the corridor, Callum is looking at a document as he bumps into Celeste. They share an eyelock for a moment however Damien says *"bro, we need to talk!"*. Celeste heads to class as Damien brings Callum to the canteen. Callum asks coldly *"what do you want Damien?"*. Damien asks, *"what's going on between you and Celeste?"*. Callum rolls his eyes replying, *"it is not any of your business!"*. Damien says, *"I know you lost your mom but hurting Celeste isn't the solution"*. Callum laughs coldly as he says, *"I can't believe you are defending her; she killed my mother!"*. Damien says, *"Celeste would never do something like that, she is a pure-kind-hearted person"*.

Callum scoffs as Damien says *"Callum, think twice what you are planning to do because if you find out that Celeste is innocent, it's going to kill you inside"*. Callum walks away as Damien thinks *'I need to prove Celeste's innocent'*. As the class begins; the teacher pairs the students for a team project as Celeste looks at Callum. Callum comes over to Celeste as she is a little frightened when she sees Damien smiling at her. Callum watches Celeste and Damien as he says, *"got yourself a new boyfriend?"*. Celeste says, *"just shut up Callum!"*. Callum tries to scare her however Celeste stands up and says, *"you can keep your dirty thoughts to yourself, I am not going to justify or explain anything!".* Celeste takes her bag and walks out of the class as Callum sees everyone looking at him as he yells *"WHAT ARE YOU LOT STARING AT!".* Meanwhile, Samara comes to the castle as Vlad lets her in, she says *" I am very sorry to hear about your loss your majesty".*

Vlad feels tired as Samara comes to the kitchen and pours her potion into a cup. She soon brings it out to Vlad who drinks it as Samara says, *"I want you to leave".* Before Samara can leave; Vlad holds her hand and stops her as he says, *" will you spend the night with me?".* Samara smirks evilly as she strokes Vlad as he hugs her. Samara thinks *' very soon you will be begging me to marry you.'* Meanwhile, at the back of the college Celeste is annoyed as Susie comes in front of her and says, *"hello sis!".* Damien sees Susie and Celeste talking as he decides to film them; Celeste coldly says, *"get out of my way Susie!".* Susie hisses at her as Celeste looks spooked as Susie taunts Celeste saying "me *and Sexyman spent the night together! Oh, so sad that you and Callum will never be together!".* Celeste is hurt however she stays strong replying *" at least I can live with myself that I didn't kill someone".* Damien wonders *'what does Celeste mean by that?'.* Susie's eyes go dark red as she brings out her fang and threatens Celeste *"if you ever think of telling Callum that I killed his mom, I will kill you!".* Susie goes as Celeste takes a deep breath. Celeste decides to go home as Damien watches the footage and says, *"this will prove Celeste's innocence".* As Celeste is almost home; she hears a noise coming from an alleyway as she goes to check it out; someone knocks her from behind and drags her away.

Chapter 31

A few hours pass as Celeste slowly opens her eyes as she feels her head hurting and looks around. She feels her hands and legs are tied up and wonders *'what happened? Where am I?'*. Elsewhere, Callum is at a bar getting drunk as Damien comes over to speak with him. Damien says "*Callum, we need to talk*". Callum says in a drunk state "*how could she kill my mom? I cared for her so much and I truly fell...*". Callum is about to fall as Damien holds him and brings him back to his place. He places Callum on the sofa as he looks at him thinking *'now is not a good time to show him the clip'*.

Callum murmurs Celeste's name and soon falls asleep. The next day Callum awakes to hold his head as Damien brings him lemon water. Callum looks at Damien and asks, "*how did I get here?*". Damien replies, "*you were drunk yesterday at the bar*". Callum drinks the water as he feels a little better; Damien says, "*there's something I need to show you*". Damien gives Callum his phone and shows the clip of Celeste and Susie. As Callum listens closely, he hears Susie's confession. Damien takes his phone back as Callum is left in shock after watching the footage. Callum says "*how could I not believe Celeste? how could I hurt her so much?*". Damien says, "*Celeste was always innocent, and you hurt her so much*". Callum remembers hurting her in the hospital and on the field as he begins to cry. Damien says "*Callum, not everything is lost! You can talk to Celeste and work things out*". Callum says, "*I can't face her...*".

Meanwhile, Celeste was still trapped as she struggled to free herself; just then the door opens as someone comes downstairs. Celeste is shocked to see who it is as they remove the tape from her mouth and she says "*you?*"; he looks at her and says "*Celeste, what are you doing here?*". Celeste asks "*Gabriel, why did you kidnap me?*". Back at Damien's place, Callum is punching the wall in anger as Damien says, "*Callum enough!*". Callum drops to the floor, Damien says "*I know you are hurting because of Celeste, but she will forgive you"*. Callum cries as he holds Damien *"I don't deserve her... she will be better off without me"*. Damien says annoyed *"don't be like that! snap out of it!"*. Damien grabs his phone and calls Celeste as Celeste feels her phone in her pocket. Gabriel takes it out as Celeste says, *"Gabriel, please answer it! I need someone to help me out"*. However, before Gabriel can answer the phone, Samara grabs it. Samara throws the phone to the wall as it breaks; Celeste angrily says " *OI, THAT'S MY PHONE!"*. Samara tells Gabriel to head upstairs as Samara turns to Celeste and says, *"don't worry Celeste, I will be back soon"*.

As Samara comes back upstairs, locking the basement door. Gabriel asks " *mom, why have you kidnapped Celeste? What are you planning to do?"*. Samara coldly says, *"mind your own business son!"*. Back at Damien's house, he has been trying to get hold of Celeste however wonders *'why is Celeste not picking up her phone? Has something happened to her?'*. Back in the basement, Celeste looks at her broken phone and wonders *'who could have called me? it wouldn't be Callum? He hates me... but despite everything why is my heart unable to hate him?'*. Elsewhere, Susie is feeding on a human as she thinks *'I better call my sexyman.. maybe he wants to hook up.'* Susie calls Callum's mobile however Damien sees her incoming call and rejects it.

Chapter 32

S usie wonders *'why is sexyman ignoring my calls, maybe I better go and see him?'*. Damien and Callum come to the castle as Damien says *"Callum, you know what you need to do tomorrow"*. Callum nods and says, *"thanks Damien for being a great friend"*. As Callum tries to get some sleep; Susie sneaks in through his window as she kisses Callum's lips and proceeds to remove his clothes. Callum awakes and pushes her off as Susie yells *"what the hell Callum!"*. Callum asks annoyed *"what are you doing here Susie?"*. Susie flirts replying, *"I've come to cheer up, let me make you forget everything"*. Callum says *"Susie, I am not in the mood and maybe we shouldn't do this"*. Susie pulls Callum closer and says, *"we had a deal"*. Callum angrily pushes Susie off as his eyes turn red. Callum says, *" I know what you did Susie, don't even try to deny it"*. Susie asks confused *"what are you talking about Sexyman?"*. Callum says, *" I know it was you who killed my mother"*.

Susie is shocked as she tries to explain and blames Celeste. Callum's eyes darken with rage as he yells *" DON'T YOU DARE BLAME CELESTE FOR YOUR ACTIONS!"*. Susie is frightened as she says *"Callum don't be like this! I am your Susie-woozy"*. Callum brings her down the castle as Elise asks *"Callum, who is she?"*. Callum throws Susie out and warns her *" if you ever come back or show your face to me again, I will kill you for good!"*. Callum slams the door as Susie thinks angrily *' I AM GOING TO KILL YOU CELESTE!'*. The next day Callum comes to college as he looks for Celeste, he checks her timetable and the campus however Celeste is not there. Callum wonders *'where could Celeste be?'*. Callum comes to Celeste's house as Elijah opens the door. Callum says, *"good afternoon, sir, is Celeste here?"*. Elijah replies *"I don't know where my no-good daughter is. probably having sex or something"*. Callum clenches his fist as he is shocked to hear how Elijah speaks about Celeste as Elijah continues to taunt Celeste. Callum's eye change to red as he beats Elijah and says *"HOW DARE YOU SPEAK ABOUT*

CELESTE LIKE THIS? DO YOU KNOW HOW SPECIAL AND HOW BEAUTIFUL SHE IS?". Elijah says " *Celeste is nothing more than a murderer to me; she killed my Amanda. Brianna is also dead.* Callum continues to beat Elijah as he yells "*CELESTE IS NOT A MURDERER! I LOVE...*". Damien comes to Callum as he says, "Callum *stop!*".

Callum leaves Elijah on the floor as they come out of the house. Damien makes a call for the ambulance to the house. Callum says, " *you should have just let me kill him*". Damien says, "*how do you think Celeste would feel if you did that? she has already lost her sisters, her mom and now you want to kill her dad?*". Callum coldly says, "when *we find Celeste, she will stay with me*". Back in the basement, Celeste was feeling hungry and weak as the door opens as Celeste says "*Gabriel, is that you?*". Samara comes down with a plate of stew and water as she says, "*only me Celeste, how are you?*". Celeste tries to free herself as she asks, "*who are you? why have you kidnapped me?*". Samara replies "*I am Samara and the reason for your capture is because of Callum*". Samara explains her plan as Celeste is shocked and says, "*you are evilly and wicked*". Samara laughs evilly as she feeds Celeste the stew however Celeste spits it over Samara. Celeste says, "*I don't want to eat your muck!*".

Samara tortures Celeste as she screams in pain; Callum feels Celeste's pain as Damien asks, "*are you ok Callum?*". Callum says, " *I felt Celeste's pain, she has been taken by someone who is hurting her?*". Damien asks, " *but who would take her?*". Callum comes to the castle with Damien as Vlad says, "*Callum is everything ok?*". Callum asks "*dad, where is Celeste?*". Vlad says, " *I thought you were dealing with her.*" Damien looks at Callum as he says, " *if your dad doesn't have Celeste...*". Vlad says, " *if you are unable to seek vengeance for your mom, maybe I should just kill her*". Callum's eyes darken as he says, "*DON'T YOU DARE TRY ANYTHING!*". Vlad is stunned to see a change in Callum as Callum says, "*Celeste didn't murder mom*". Back in the basement, Celeste lay unconscious as Samara came upstairs and locked the door. Gabriel watched his mom leave as he saw the basement door and thought *'poor Celeste, she doesn't deserve this.'*

Chapter 33

Gabriel makes a sandwich in the kitchen as he opens the lock to the basement. He comes downstairs as Celeste felt weak; Gabriel says *"Celeste, you need to eat"*. He feeds Celeste as she eats hungrily. Gabriel says, *"I guess, you love peanut butter and jelly"*. Celeste says, "I haven't had a decent meal in days". As Gabriel gives her some juice; Celeste says *"Gabriel, please help me"*. Gabriel looks at Celeste as he soon heads upstairs. Celeste thinks *'please Callum wherever you are, help me!'*. Back at the castle, Vlad and Callum were arguing as Vlad says *" how can you be so sure she didn't kill your mother? Your feelings have clouded your judgment!"*. Callum angrily fights his father *" I KNOW CELESTE WOULD NEVER HARM ANYONE!"*. Damien soon stops Callum as Vlad's eye changes to rage red as he says *" if I find Celeste before you! I will kill her!"*. Vlad leaves the castle as Callum looks at Damien. Damien says *"Callum, we need to find Celeste"*. Elsewhere Vlad feeds on a human and kills him; Vlad thinks *' I will find that human girl and kill her'*. Meanwhile, Samara was making a potion as Gabriel came into the room; Samara asks, *"what is it, Gabriel?"*. Gabriel says *" mom, can you let Celeste go? why is she still being held captive?"*. Samara laughs evilly replying *" she is the golden ticket... I am going to negotiate something with Callum for higher power!"*.

Samara sends Gabriel outside as she finishes making her potion. Gabriel thinks *'I need to help Celeste'*. As Samara leaves the hut, Gabriel waits for a few moments before unlocking the door. Meanwhile, Vlad is on a killing spree in the woods as Samara sets her plan in action; Samara drinks a potion as she changes into Carmilla's form. Vlad sees her and says, *"my love, you are alive"*. She comes closer to him and pushes Vlad into a corner and ties a silver chain around the tree trapping him. Vlad touches the silver as he screams in agony; Carmilla says coldly *"you couldn't avenge my death! You couldn't fulfil my wish"*. Vlad says, *"my love, don't leave me"*. Carmilla comes into the silver chain as she passionately kisses Vlad who pins her against the tree; Carmilla whispers into his ears ' *avenge my death! Kill the girl'.*

Carmilla comes out as Vlad's eyes change to purple as he says in a trance *" I will avenge you, my love"*. Back at Samara's hut, Gabriel frees Celeste as she stands up weakly. However just as they come upstairs; Samara sees Gabriel holding Celeste as she says, *"What do you think you are doing?"*. Gabriel says *"mom, please let her go"*. Samara chants a spell which makes Celeste and Gabriel feel weak; Samara pushes Celeste back downstairs, tying her up as Gabriel whimpers *"mom...please"*. Samara lets the spell go as Gabriel drops to the floor trying to catch his breath. Samara warns him *" IF YOU TRY TO HELP THE GIRL ESCAPE! I WILL KILL YOU UNDERSTAND!"*. Gabriel nods as he heads upstairs; meanwhile, Callum and Damien are searching around the town for Celeste however Callum soon falls to the ground as Damien comes over to him asking *"are you ok?"*. Callum replies *"yes, but I think I felt a stronger pain from Celeste.. whoever has her I won't spare them"*. Back in the woods, Vlad fights the silver chain despite his injuries and follows a scent thinking ' *I will complete my mission, I will kill Celeste'.* Back in the basement, Celeste takes a deep breath as she thinks ' *I need to escape no matter what.*

Chapter 34

Celeste struggles to free herself as Samara comes downstairs; Samara says, " *I will make sure you get punished for escaping*". Celeste says, "*I still don't know why you have kept me here*". Samara says "*you are special.. but I will see how you will survive against an attack from the Vampire King*". Celeste is confused and asks, "*why are you doing this?*". Samara laughs evilly as she says, " *I don't have to answer to you! but I will tell you one thing, your fate will end up like Carmilla*". Samara tortures Celeste and leaves the room; Celeste thinks weakly '*could Samara has been the reason why Carmilla was killed?*'. Meanwhile, later that night Damien and Callum came to a bar. Callum drank a few glasses of whiskey as he says "*Celeste, my love where are you?*". Damien tries to help Callum control himself as he says, " *I am going to head to the bathroom, don't go anywhere*". As Damien leaves, Susie comes over to Callum as she says "*sexyman, let me take away all your pain*".

Callum looks at Susie who strokes his face; for a moment Callum sees Celeste smiling at him. Callum says, "*you came back*". Susie kisses Callum passionately as Callum pulls her closer; Damien comes back as he pushes Susie off Callum as Susie angrily says, " *WHAT THE HELL!*". Damien holds Callum who says "*what happened? where's Celeste?*". Damien says "*Susie, if you try to come between Celeste and Callum, I will end you*". Susie snarls angrily as she leaves. Damien brings Callum back to the castle as Callum asks, "*where's Celeste?*". Damien puts Callum to sleep as he takes Celeste's name. Damien thinks ' *Cel, where are you?*'. Back in Samara's hut, Gabriel wonders '*how am I going to help Celeste?*'. Vlad is in the woods as Samara comes downstairs. She unties Celeste's hand and says, "*you are free to leave*". Celeste runs upstairs as she grabs a mobile and leaves the hut; Celeste looks around the wood as she runs and dials Damien's mobile number.

It begins to ring as Celeste stops when she sees a shadowy figure looking at her. Celeste says "*Callum, is that you?*". Vlad walks through the mist with red eyes looking at her evilly; Celeste panics as she runs in the opposite direction. Damien sees an incoming private number and answers *"hello".* Celeste says *"Damien...".* Damien says " *Celeste, where are you? are you ok?".* Celeste hides behind a tree and tries to update Damien as Vlad comes in front of her. Vlad says *"YOU KILLED MY WIFE! NOW I WILL KILL YOU AND AVENGE HER!".* Celeste says worriedly, *"please don't hurt me".* Vlad tries to attack her as a purple blast pushes him against the tree, Celeste closes her eyes as she falls to the ground. Damien says *"hello Cel..".* Samara comes to the unconscious Celeste as she smirks evilly; she takes the phone as Samara says *"Damien... what happened?".* Damien says " *Hannah? Is Celeste with you? where are you?".*

Samara replies " *Damien... I am so scared.. I don't know where I am".* Damien says, *"send me your location through the phone".* Samara replies " *I don't know how to do it.. save me".* Samara screams as she ends the call. Damien panics " *hello? Hannah?".* Samara sees the unconscious Vlad as she says " *you're completely useless! At least with your wife she did my bidding until I had to kill her".* Samara puts a spell that takes Celeste away from the woods. The next morning Callum awakes as Damien says, " *I spoke with Celeste last night, but whoever has her also has Hannah too".* Damien thinks about Hannah as Callum says, *"we will find them both".* Back in a bedroom, Vlad begins to open his eyes as he looks around trying to remember how he got there. Samara comes over wearing black lingerie as he says *"what happened? How did I get here?".* Samara pretends to act sadly as she replies, " *last night, don't you remember... we made love?".* Vlad is shocked as he says " *what?... no, I would never do that to Carmilla".* Samara cries and says, *"maybe I should kill myself".* Vlad stops her as Samara gives him a drink which makes him under her spell. Vlad says *"sweetheart, I will make you my wife".* Samara hugs Vlad as she smirks evilly thinking *'my next attack will be on Callum'.*

Chapter 35

Celeste awoke to find herself tied up again as she felt a sharp pain in her head; she wondered, *'what happened last night? I remember leaving here... but'*. Celest panics remembering Vlad's red eyes; meanwhile, Callum and Damien were both trying to track down Celeste's phone. Callum got impatient as he asks, *"how long is it going to take Damien?"*. Damien sighed as he replies, *"I am working on it"*. Later that afternoon, Samara brings Vlad back to the castle as she is about to leave however Vlad holds her hand. Samara turns back as she smiles at Vlad who kisses her hand and says *"Sweetheart, please don't leave me"*. Samara hugs him as she replies, *"I am not going to leave you, babe"*. Meanwhile, Gabriel manages to escape from his room as he thinks *'I need to tell Callum where Celeste is'*. Gabriel calls Callum's phone as Callum sees an incoming call from Gabriel as Callum says, *"why is this loser calling me?"*. Callum ignores all of Gabriel's calls as Gabriel thinks for a moment and then dials Damien's number.

Damien picks up as he says *"Gabriel, we are a little busy at the moment"*. Gabriel says, *"I know you are looking for Celeste, I know where she is"*. Damien says, *"can you meet us in the college library asap?"*. Gabriel replies *"ok, I am on my way"*. Callum looks at Damien asking, *"what did Gabriel want?"*. Damien replies *"we need to get to the library now!"*. Back at the castle, Samara began plans for the wedding as she invited everyone; in another room, Samara brewed a potion as she thought *'this will destroy Callum'*. A few moments later, Damien and Callum come to the library as Gabriel sees them. Damien asks *"Gabriel, you said you had some news on Celeste... and what about Hannah?"*. As Callum looks at Gabriel with a worried expression; Gabriel says, *"I want you guys to promise that you won't hurt me, I tried to help Celeste escape, but she didn't let me"*. Callum replies *"who didn't let you?"*. Gabriel replies *"Samara, she is behind Celeste's kidnapping"*. Callum's eyes widen with anger as he thinks *'how dare that witch take my girl?'*. Damien

73

asks, "*can you take us to Celeste?*". Gabriel nods as they follow him out into the corridor; Susie corners Callum against the locker as she says " *hey sexyman*". Callum pushes her off as Susie looks angry and annoyed. Callum says " *leave me alone Susie! I don't love you*". Susie's eye changes to red in rage as she says " *how dare you to try to play with my feelings Sexyman? you think Celeste will want you after knowing we have slept together and had an intimate relationship*". Callum holds Susie by her throat as she begins to choke; Callum says, " *if you ever try to come between me and Celeste, I will end you!*". Damien comes in as he says, "*Callum bro, come on we need to go*".

Back in the basement, Celeste closes her eyes and opens her mind as she remembers Carmilla's last words. Celeste opens her eyes as she thinks '*I need to tell Callum what Carmilla told me*'. Back at the castle, Samara had already begun with the decorations as Vlad came over to her. Samara asks " *when will Callum be back? I wouldn't want him to miss our vows*". Vlad kisses Samara replying, " *I am sure he will be back soon my love*". Meanwhile, Elise watches them upstairs as she remembered seeing Samara in the room acting strange; Elise comes back into the room, and she sees the blue liquid in a bottle. Elise thinks ' *I better inform Callum about this*'. Elise tries to mind-link to Callum. Elsewhere, Damien and Gabriel are close to the hut as Callum senses the mind-link and answers "*sis, is everything ok?*". Elise replies, "*Callum, you need to come home! Samara is planning to marry daddy and she is being very strange*". Inside the hut, Gabriel breaks the lock as he runs downstairs where Damien sees Celeste in a very weak state. Damien says "*Celeste, don't worry. We are going to get you out*". Damien carries Celeste out of the hut as Callum sees Celeste and strokes her forehead. Callum says "*Damien, you need to get her to the hospital*". Gabriel notices that Callum has a deep expression says "*Callum, what is going on?*". Callum has a serious look on his face as he says "*Gabriel, I am going to need your help*". Gabriel nods as they all leave from the woods.

Chapter 36

They bring Celeste to the hospital as she lays on the bed; the doctor comes in and examines her. Callum looks at Celeste through the glass as he says, "*please be ok Celeste, I don't know what I would do without you*". Damien puts a hand on his shoulder and says, "*don't worry bro, she will be ok.*" Callum hugs Damien as he says, "*I've got to go but keep an eye on her please*". Damien nods as Callum leaves; he wonders ' *where is Callum going?*'. Callum was near the castle as he thought '*I need to see Elise and talk to her*'. Back at the hospital, Damien and Gabriel have a talk as Gabriel says, "*I am sorry for everything, I mean Celeste getting kidnapped was my mother's fault*". Damien says, "*you are not to blame and if anything, Samara is an evil witch*". Gabriel feels more apologetic as Damien says "*hey, you brought Celeste to safety, and I know you did try to help her escape*". Gabriel soon wipes a tear from his eye. Damien asks "*Gabriel, did Callum tell you what's up?*". Gabriel shakes his head confused as he replies, " *no what is up?*".

Back at the castle, Samara was adding the final touches to the drink. She held up the goblet and said, "*poor Callum after drinking this he will be dead*". Elise films Samara however Samara sees a reflection in the mirror and turns as she asks, "*what are you doing little one?*". Elise says coldly, "*you think you're going to marry my daddy well you're not and you will not hurt my brother either!*". Elise shows her fangs as Samara says, "*hand over your phone now!*". Elise tries to run out however Samara grabs her and drags her to the dungeons. Samara snatches the phone as she smashes it as Elise looks scared; Samara threatens Elise as she says, "*you be a good girl and not get in my way; in return I might spare your life*". Samara soon heads upstairs leaving Elise alone as she cries and thinks '*Callum it's up to you now*'.

Callum arrives home as Vlad says, "*son you're back*". Callum smiles as he says, "*yeah we found Celeste, but she is in the hospital*". Vlad says, " *there is something we need to talk about Callum*". Callum was surprised as he asked *"yeah sure dad, but first where's Elise? I need to talk to her"*. Samara comes out of the kitchen holding three glasses of juice; Samara says, *"hello Callum, I have prepared a special drink for us"*. Samara hands a juice to Vlad as Callum looks at Vlad asking *"dad, what is she doing here?"*. Vlad replies *"son don't be so rude; she is allowed to be here"*. Samara hands Callum a drink as she says, *"you must be thirsty Callum have a drink"*. As Callum took the drink in his hands; he looked at the cup as he thought *'why would Samara make this drink? what is she playing at?'*. As Vlad drinks his juice, he notices Callum hasn't taken a sip as Callum says, *"I am going to head upstairs and rest I will have it later"*. Samara scowls as Callum heads upstairs to his room and thinks *'I hope he drinks it soon otherwise the potion won't work!'*.

Chapter 37

As Callum sits in his room looking at the goblet and wonders '*what is Samara's plan?*'. Callum looks at a plant as he pours the liquid in the plant; Callum watches for a moment as the plant slowly dies. Callum thinks '*what the hell! Samara tried to poison me.*' Back downstairs, Samara places an arm around Vlad as she says "*I hope you are excited about tomorrow as I am babes.* Vlad and Samara share a kiss as Callum watches his dad from behind the wall thinking '*Samara has to be manipulating dad!*'. Back in the dungeon, Elise tries to call for her help as she screams "*HELP SOMEONE PLEASE SAVE ME!*". Elise cries as she prays '*Callum please find me soon.*' Callum soon comes into the living room as he says, "*I'm hungry*". Samara was stunned to see Callum all ok as she wonders '*did Callum drink the potion? If he did then why is he still alive?*'. Callum waves his hand as Samara smiles "*I will go and prepare it, dear*". Vlad follows Samara around like a lovesick puppy to the kitchen.

Meanwhile, back at the hospital, Gabriel and Damien were sitting in Celeste's room. Gabriel looks at Celeste as he thinks ' *please wake up soon Celeste, we are all worried*'. Damien's stomach growls as Gabriel laughs as Damien says, "*I will get us some snacks*". Gabriel nods as Damien leaves the room; he heads to the canteen however as he comes back, he is stunned to see Susie. Damien walks over to her and asks, "*what are you doing here?*". Susie rolls her eyes as she asks, "*is Callum here?*". Damien looks at her with a cold expression as he says, "*I've already told you that you and Callum will never happen.*" Susie says, " *I love him and he's my sexyman*". Damien's eyes turn red as he says angrily "*DON'T YOU GET IT THROUGH YOUR DUMB BRAIN! CELESTE AND CALLUM ARE SOULMATES!*". Susie is frightened as a nurse comes and says, "*can you please quieten down?*". Damien points at the window as Susie sees Celeste unconscious and soon leaves.

Gabriel opens the door to see Damien and asks, "*what was going on?*". Damien comes in with the snacks as he tells Gabriel what happened. Back at the castle, later that evening Samara came downstairs holding a tray of food as she opened the dungeon as Elise turned to look at Samara with coldness and fear in her eyes. Samara says, "*poor little one, I have brought you some food*". Elise shivers as she says, " *please let me go, I promise I won't tell Callum anything*". Samara says in a fake pity tone " *aww poor Elise, see I would love to trust you but until my wedding to Vlad doesn't happen! You will need to stay down here*". Samara leaves as Elise cries and feels alone; Callum sees Samara soon leave the dungeons and wonders '*what is Samara hiding?*'. Back at the hospital, Celeste has a strange vision as she awakes and screams "*CALLUM!*".

Chapter 38

C eleste soon lays back down and closes her eyes; she drifts off into dreamland. In her mind, she thinks about her mom and sister; Celeste looks around and finds herself in a forest as she sees Samara killing her mom. Celeste panics as she begins to cry when someone comes over to her and taps her shoulder "*do not cry, dear*". Celeste looked up to see it was Carmilla as Celeste says " *Samara, she killed my mom... and*". Carmilla shakes her head replying, " *me too... but you need to be brave because Callum needs you*". Celeste says " *I can't defeat her... I am ordinary*". Carmilla says " *you are far from ordinary Celeste, you are special... you have a gift, and you are my son's soulmate*". Carmilla shows Celeste a memory from her childhood as Celeste is surprised to see her younger self. Carmilla says " *I will let you go... you will need to help Callum but remember the words I told you*". Celeste was confused by Carmilla's riddle talk as Carmilla soon disappeared. Back in the hospital, Celeste was tossing and turning as Gabriel says "*Damien, get the doctor!*". Damien nodded as he ran out and called for the nurses and doctor to check on Celeste. Gabriel held Celeste's hand as he says, "*come on Celeste, you need to wake up*". Damien soon returns with the doctor who examines Celeste and says, "*she's traumatized from what happened, however, she will recover*".

Meanwhile, back at the castle, Callum thought '*what is Samara hiding in the dungeons?*'. Callum came to the door as Samara saw him and asks "*Callum, where are you going?*". Callum asks, " *what are you hiding in there Samara?*". Samara laughs as she replies, " *I just like checking on the rats*". Callum looks at her and heads back to his room; Samara heads to the living room wearing red sexy lingerie as she says, " *Hey my sexy Vamp*". Vlad says, "*come over here sexy!*". Samara puts on a sexy song as she pounces on Vlad as kisses him passionately as Vlad pushes her against the wall not breaking their kiss. Samara wraps her legs around Vlad as Samara whispers in his ears '*show me what you are made of'.* Vlad lifts her and carries her to the bedroom as Samara thinks ' *soon my plan will be completed'.* Later that afternoon, Samara calls Gabriel as she says, " *hey Gabriel, is Celeste still locked up in the hut?".* Gabriel replies " *I don't know mom... remember you put a lock and warned me not to go downstairs".* Samara rolls her eyes and says "*ok, I will head over and check".* Gabriel hangs up the phone as he looks at Damien with a worried expression. Damien asks, " *what is it, Gabriel?".* Gabriel replies " *my mom's going to look for Celeste".* Damien looks at Celeste and says, " *we need to protect her until Callum comes back".* Gabriel nods.

As the evening falls, Samara heads back to the hut as she opens the basement to find Celeste was gone and screamed "*YOU WILL NOT ESCAPE ME!".* Samara transforms into Hannah and calls Damien. Damien answers, "*Hannah, are you ok?".* Hannah says, " *where are you, Damien? did you find Celeste?".* Damien says "*Hannah, let's meet up".* Damien gives Hannah some directions as she soon hangs up. Gabriel comes over to Damien as he says "*Damien, I don't know why but I feel like there's something off about Hannah".* Damien says, *"you're just acting weird; I love Hannah and I trust her".* Back at the hut, Hannah smirks evilly and leaves, back in the castle Callum knocks on Vlad's room as Vlad says "*enter".* Callum sees the room with candles and rose petals as he feels grossed out as Vlad asks, *"can I help you son?".* Callum shakes his head as he leaves and heads to the hospital. Callum comes into the room and takes Celeste's hand as he asks " *Damien, Gabriel did Celeste wake up? what did the doctors say?".*

Chapter 39

Damien updates Callum as the door opens; Callum is stunned to see Isabelle and Darren as Isabelle comes over to Celeste and asks Callum *"what happened to Celeste?"*. Callum replies *"she was kidnapped, and I brought her here"*. Isabelle sits beside Celeste as Darren says, *"you shouldn't have shut us out Callum"*. Gabriel says *"Callum, my mom is at the hut, and she has already noticed Celeste is gone"*. Callum says, *"don't leave Celeste's room and make sure you keep in contact and let me know what is happening"*. Gabriel nods as Callum says, *"Darren can we talk?"*. They head out of the room as Callum says, *" I am sorry for not telling you about Celeste, but I need your help"*. Darren replies, *" of course bro, what do you need me to do?"*. Callum updates Darren on Samara as Darren says, *"she feels like a Gabriella to me"*. Callum was confused as Darren says, *" Gabriella was the same monster who turned me and tried to harm Isabelle"*. Callum says, *" Samara is evil to the core, she tried to poison me, and she's trapped my dad"*. Darren asks, *" ok so what's the plan?"*.

Callum talks with Darren about a plan; meanwhile, Hannah comes to the hospital as she pulls Gabriel into another room. Gabriel says *"Hannah, what a surprise to see you here!"*. Hannah transforms back into Samara as Gabriel is stunned and says, *" I knew there was something fishy about you; mom, you need to stop hurting Callum and Celeste"*. Samara laughs evilly as she replies, *"you can't stop me, son!"*. Samara chanted a spell to attack Gabriel however Gabriel escaped as the room had a small explosion. Gabriel ran to find Damien as Damien asks *" Gabriel, are you ok?"*. Gabriel says *"Damien, Hannah is Samara"*. Damien was confused by Gabriel as Hannah saw Damien. Damien ran over and hugged Hannah who gave a scary look to Gabriel. Elsewhere, Callum brings Darren to the castle as Darren asks *"so what are we doing first? Do we save your dad or...?"*. Callum shows him a door to the dungeons as Callum says, "*Samara is hiding something down here and we need to find out what it is*".

Darren takes a torch; back at the hospital Hannah breaks Damien's heart as she leaves; Callum looks out of the window and sees the backyard decorated as Vlad says "*I want everything to be perfect*". Back at the hospital, Celeste awakes as Isabelle says "*doctor, Celeste is awake*". Celeste looks around as she says, "*we need to go*". Damien asks "*why?*". elsewhere, Darren soon reaches the ground floor as he opens the locked room to see a young girl crying. Elise says, "*who are you? have you come to hurt me?*". Darren mind-links Callum who rushes downstairs as Elise hugs Callum. Elise says, "*please save me, Callum*". Callum assures Elise she is safe as Elise explains how she was locked as Callum's eyes widen in anger and change to red. Callum says angrily " *I WILL DESTROY SAMARA!*". They soon head back upstairs, as in a bedroom Samara is wearing a white dress as she looks at Carmilla's photo and says "*sister, finally I will have what I deserved all these years!*".

Chapter 40

Samara finishes her makeup as she looks in the mirror with an evil smirk. As Callum, Darren, and Elise head upstairs; Callum tells Elise to change and head to the backyard. Darren and Callum come to the kitchen as Darren grabs a jar of honey and Callum grabs a pillow. Samara comes out of the room as she says, *"Callum what a surprise to see you here! how do I look?"*. Elsewhere over the hill, Celeste was with her friends as they were headed towards the castle. However, Celeste soon stopped when she saw Susie. Isabelle asks, *"who is she?"*. Susie says *"yeah, Celeste who am I?"*. Celeste says, *"let me pass Susie"*. Susie laughed coldly saying *"you're not going to take my sexyman away from me!"*. Gabriel looks at her and says, *"you really are a delusional person... oops dead person"*. Isabelle says *"she's a Vampire! I will stake her!"*. Celeste stops Isabelle as Damien says, *"look Susie, I have already told you that Celeste and Callum are soulmates"*. Susie answers *"Callum will soon see that me and him belong together"*. Celeste sighs as she says *"Susie, look I don't want to fight you. you're my sister and I love you"*. Susie looks at her with a cold expression and says, *"you are trying to steal Callum away from me!"*. Celeste shakes her head *"no, I am not, and I would never come between you or anyone else. But Callum loves someone else! You need to stop acting crazy"*. Susie begins to cry as she says, *"if mom and Brianna were still here..."*. Susie begins to feel her humanity returning as she continues, *"I am so sorry Celeste... I have been acting crazy"*.

Celeste and Susie share a hug as Damien says *"Susie, we need your help to stop Samara"*. Susie nods as they all head up to the castle. Back inside, Samara is still flaunting herself as Darren says, *"I am sure your dress goes with anything"*. Samara says, *"of course it does..."*. Darren dumps the honey over Samara as Callum rips a pillow and blows feather all over her. Samara screams *"AAAAAAAAAAAAAAAAAAAAAAAAAAAAAAAAAAHHHHH! YOU RUINED MY DRESS! YOU BRATS!"*. Samara heads back to her room as Darren and Callum high-five each other. Darren says, "*now what do we do?*". Callum replies " *we need to head to the backyard*". Darren and Callum come to the backyard as Vlad asks, " *where's my beautiful bride?*". Callum says, " *dad you need to snap out of it!*". Darren laughs as Callum shoots him a death glare. Celeste comes in the backyard as she says " *Callum... let me try*". Callum turns hearing Celeste's voice as Callum steps back from his dad; Celeste closes her eyes as Vlad feels a little tingling as Celeste opens her eyes again. Vlad looks around as he says, " *what is going on? where am I?*". Elise runs to Vlad and hugs him saying "*daddy you're back*". Samara comes as she says " *OK, I'm ready to get married, my sexy Vampire*". Vlad asks, "*what are you doing here Samara? what are you talking about?*". Samara smiles as she replies, " *it's our wedding day sweetheart*". Vlad coldly says, "*I'm loyal to Carmilla, even if she is not in this world anymore*".

Samara was shocked by Vlad's response as she felt her magic spell had been broken; Celeste says "*Samara, your days are over! You murdered Carmilla and my mother*". Everyone gasps as Samara say " *what are you talking about? I would never hurt my own sister*". Celeste says "*don't even try to deny it! I have proof*". Celeste uses her power to create a portal to show the past however as Celeste begins to feel weak and falls, Isabelle and Damien hold her; she sees a familiar face who uses a spell on Samara who confesses " *YES IT WAS ME! I KILLED CARMILLA! I WANTED POWER AND MORE.... I KILLED CELESTE'S MOTHER... I WANTED TO BE THE MOST POWERFUL WITCH IN THE WORLD! I ALSO PLAYED WITH DAMIEN'S FEELINGS BY PRETENDING TO BE HANNAH TO SPLIT UP CELESTE AND CALLUM*".

Celeste smiles seeing her mother's spirit who soon goes as Samara stops talking. Vlad looks angry at her " *YOU DISGUSTING WITCH! YOU TOOK THE LOVE OF MY LIFE FOR POWER! YOU'RE SICK AND MENTAL*". Samara goes to attack Celeste and says, " *YOU ARE TO BLAME FOR THIS!*". Celeste manages to use a little energy she has left and traps Samara in an hourglass as Samara bangs *'LET ME OUT'.* Celeste collapses as Callum comes over to her. Gabriel feels her pulse and says, *"she needs to rest".* Callum carries her inside and puts her on the couch. Vlad takes the hourglass as he comes down to the dungeons and puts her in a cell. Vlad says, *" you trapped my little girl in here for days! now this dungeon will be your new home for all eternity".* Elise laughs and says *" you meanie! You deserve this".* Susie calls the doctor who examines Celeste stating, *" she will be ok! she needs to rest".* Callum takes Celeste's hand and kisses it. Isabelle and Darren share a kiss as Damien, Gabriel, and Susie leave. A few days pass as Celeste recovers as she spends time with Callum. Callum brings Celeste to the college sports field as he has a special surprise for her. Callum gets down on his knee as he says *" Celeste being with you makes me feel alive. When I lost you I felt trapped, alone, and lifeless; I can't imagine my life without you. I love you; will you marry me?".*

Celeste has tears in her eyes as she nods and kisses Callum who lifts her in his arms. Fireworks explode in the sky as everyone celebrates and congratulates the happy couple. Isabelle says *"bestie, I can't wait for your wedding. who knows maybe our kids will become besties?".* Darren congratulates Callum saying *" bro, it's about time you settled down, I wish you and Celeste all the happiness".* Susie hugs Celeste happily as she turns to leave when Damien stops her and says *" Susie, I know you are probably wishing for a sexyman, but I think deep down you are a beautiful girl....".* Susie is confused as she asks, *" Damien what are you trying to ask me?".* Damien feels a little flustered as Gabriel comes up behind him and says, *"I think he's trying to ask you out".* Susie smiles as she nods replying *" as friends though?".* Damien says, *" whatever you want Susie!".*

They share a smile. Three years later, Celeste and Callum are happily married with a son named Silas. Back in the castle, Callum has taken over from his dad as the Vampire King; Susie and Darren are happily married with a daughter Alessia. Later that evening, Celeste is looking at the sky as she holds Silas in her arms as Silas says, *"there are so many stars in the sky mommy"*. Celeste says, " *the two shining stars are your grandmas... watching you always"*. There is a knock on the door as Celeste opens to see a young girl running in as she says, "*Silas let's play hide and seek"*. Celeste says "*Gracie, it's almost bedtime"*. Isabelle and Darren come in as Celeste greet them. The kids play in the garden as Celeste catches up with Isabelle and Darren; Callum soon comes by as he kisses Celeste. Celeste says, " *could you ever imagine that life would bring us here today?"*. Isabelle holds Darren's hand and says, " *our love is eternal and everlasting"*. Callum says to Celeste " *I will forever always be by your side... you and Silas are my everything"*. Vlad comes out with Elise as Elise says, " *we need to capture the memory"*. Gracie and Silas run to their parents as Elise takes a group selfie.

Lightning Source UK Ltd.
Milton Keynes UK
UKHW012017180422
401702UK00003B/50